COWTOWN KIDNAP

When Slim Petersen overhears kidnap plans, involving the son of one of the Vargo boys, he fails to convince the brothers of the plot — until there's an attempt upon his own life. Then, despite him working to thwart the kidnappers, it seems that the outlaws' plans are working. One Vargo dies and another is taken prisoner. Slim has help when he faces the renegades in a final, explosive showdown. Men die and he frees the prisoner — but can he survive?

DAVID BINGLEY

COWTOWN KIDNAP

Complete and Unabridged

LINFORD
Leicester

First published in Great Britain in 1971

London

First Linford Edition
published 2010

British Library CIP Data

Bingley, David, *1920* –
    Cowtown kidnap. - -
    (Linford western library)
    1. Western stories.
    2. Large type books.
    I. Title II. Series
    823.9'14–dc22

    ISBN 978–1–44480–396–9

Published by
F. A. Thorpe (Publishing)
Anstey, Leicestershire

Set by Words & Graphics Ltd.
Anstey, Leicestershire
Printed and bound in Great Britain by
T. J. International Ltd., Padstow, Cornwall

This book is printed on acid-free paper

1

The air in the Painted Desert saloon was far from clean. At one o'clock in the afternoon, upwards of a score of hard-drinking, hard-smoking men were bellied up to the long bar, or sprawled in chairs around the nearest tables. Smoke climbed towards the darkened ceiling from three pipes, a couple of cigars and half a dozen cigarettes.

Through the windows, the main street of Medicine Creek was showing a heat haze which played tricks with the eyes of the drinking men. Very few people were on the street at that time. Some of the townsfolk were eating, while others were seeking the shade and taking what rest they could afford in the heat of the day.

Mostly the drinkers in the saloon were in small groups. One young cowpuncher, around the narrow end of

1

the bar, however, was solemnly licking his lips and contemplating the inch of beer at the bottom of his fourth pint of the tepid liquid. He had a half smile on his broad mouth, and his expression suggested that he had all the company he wanted inside the glass.

Slim Petersen, for that was his name, had not spent any length of time in a saloon for over two months. Quite recently he had travelled south to a ranch over the border, in Texas. He had been returning from a cattle drive mounted by his boss to a distant town in the state of Kansas. Now, he was in Clovis County, east central New Mexico territory, with his wages in his pocket. He was on his way to visit the home of the man who had raised him. He had not been near the man in question for five years.

Slim was a restless, freckled, sandy-haired fellow of twenty-three years. His face was cleanshaven, apart from long tapering sideburns. He had lazy blue eyes which were deceptive, and good

2

widely-spaced teeth which often showed because of his frequent smiles.

He finished off the drink, stroked his forehead above the bleached brows with a broad whiskered hand, and casually eased back his weathered, side-rolled dun hat. A brown paper cigarette was burning close to his fingers. He examined it, decided that he had no further use for it, and rubbed out the butt on his boot heel.

The heat of the day and the half gallon of beer were having a profound effect upon him. He smiled to himself. Before he left Farwell, on the Texas side of the border, he had promised himself that he would not tarry to regail himself until he had reached Pop Legrange's homestead in Nester Valley. And here he was, scarcely half a day's ride from the place and swilling beer.

He thought that the spirit had been willing, but the flesh weak. Not that the weakness added up to anything. A man only recently relieved of the chores of cattle driving had a good deal to put

3

back into his body in the way of moisture.

He rubbed a pointed boot toe against the front of the bar and contemplated the immediate future. It had been his intention to go to the best cafe in town and partake of a long and leisurely meal, but his intake of beer now made that seem rather pointless.

He craved sleep before food. He yawned to himself, and studied the morose features of a couple of cattle ranchers who were arguing about the difficulties of running a large spread in these trying days. Slim reckoned that as long as there were men to hire themselves out for thirty dollars a month and food, the ranchers would continue to prosper without too much personal effort.

He put a coin on the counter, touched his hat to no one in particular and sauntered through the tables towards the batwings, intent upon an hour's sleep in the pleasantest free spot he could find.

The benches on either side of the street along the central part of Main Street were already occupied by regular siesta takers. Slim paused on the sidewalk, his hat pushed back and his thumbs tucked in his belt. He grinned. If they liked sleeping on benches close to a smelly dirty street, that was all right for them. But not for him.

He strolled along the sidewalk to the hitch rail where he had left his muscular dun horse. It was pestered by one or two horse flies, otherwise it had taken no harm. It shifted its hooves and rolled its neck at him as he approached, obviously wondering what he had in mind for the heat of the day.

Slim clicked his tongue. He unhitched the animal, tightened the saddle, and put himself on its back with lithe movements born of long practice. As the dun backed away from the rail, Slim hesitated for a moment, not quite sure which way he wanted to take. Medicine Creek had not received a visit from him in a long time. He had to think for a moment about its outskirts.

Finally, he turned westward, continued in that direction for a block and then turned north. Five minutes easy riding brought him to a fine thick belt of timber, lush with foliage. The grass under the trees was a fine sight to both horse and man. The man, however, looked up into the trees. There were many with low hanging branches, swaying slightly in a gentle breeze.

For as long as he could remember, Slim had been drawn to trees. He could almost always sleep well in the open, but where other men preferred to curl up on the ground, he — given the opportunity, — preferred to take his rest in a forked branch.

He picked his spot about four oaks along, but before he did anything about his rest, he dismounted and walked the dun into a grassed hollow some seventy yards away. Having slackened the saddle again, and done all he could to make it comfortable, he came back to the tree which he had picked out and studied it afresh.

He pulled off his spurs, and tossed them down in the grass some yards away. After also unloading his single right-handed Colt, he sprang up, caught the forked limb and casually hauled himself up, arms first and then legs.

A good three or four minutes were spent in finding the right section of the limb. He found it, tested it for its spring, and began to spread himself out along it, on his back. The main branch was quite a stout one, but lesser branches, growing out of the main one, had far more give in them and were consequently less safe.

Slim adjusted his hat, shifted his backbone a little way to one side and at once began to settle down. Here and there, leaves brushed him, but they did not disturb. His eyelids were heavy. The slight movement of the branch lulled him as a ship's swaying lulls sailors.

His breathing deepened but stayed noiseless.

★ ★ ★

The two men who approached the same spot fifteen minutes later came from the west. They and their horses were covered in trail dust. One of them had ridden that day much further than the other, but as neither cared very much about his appearance it was hard to tell which had done the longer distance.

The man on the bay gelding was a thick set, swarthy fellow with thick black greasy hair. His pockmarked skin and red-veined eyes made him look rather older than his forty years. He was the one who first checked his horse and looked around, while his active jaws worked on a chew of tobacco.

He said: 'Jake, you're a patient jasper when you have to be. I figure we ought to slide out of leather right here an' have that talk. Once we hit town we might get distracted there with the beer or food. What do you say?'

Jake chuckled. 'I've been hopin' to

get out of this saddle for quite a while now. It's only the prospects of spending a few hours in a town that made me keep goin' this far. Okay, so we take a short rest in the shade. And we have that talk.'

Butch Logan, the swarthy man, was the first to dismount. He rested his arms across the saddle, watching his partner dismount and wondering if he had changed at all during the months they had parted.

Jake Wagner was the taller of the two, topping six feet by a good couple of inches. He had grey, expressionless eyes, rather flat features and no brows to speak of. The only thing which made him stand out among his fellows, apart from the eyes, was a bright strip of animal hide which served as a band around his high-crowned hat.

Side by side, the partners slackened off and rocked their saddles. Jake produced the makings from the breast pocket of his shirt and Butch, meanwhile, threw himself down in the grass

9

and slaked his thirst with the contents of his water canteen. Jake rolled smokes for them both. He was still busy when he started to talk, immediately under the tree where Slim Petersen was resting.

'I kind of hope you have some encouragin' news, Butch, 'cause between you an' me, I've been havin' a lean time this last few months. Things ain't been really good for me since Doublejack Murphy was operatin' his Wild Bunch, an' you know there's a lot of water gone down to the sea since Murphy was put away.'

Logan accepted the smoke, and provided a match for both of them. He was smiling broadly and showing his tobacco-stained teeth as Jake's cigarette end first glowed red.

'Am I right in thinkin' that you'd welcome the reappearance of Doublejack Murphy, Jake?'

'Too darned right you are, amigo. The jaspers I've been ridin' with lately ain't got the right sort of attitude towards raidin' to make it a profitable pastime. Besides, the way they do it, it ain't safe enough. But why did you ask that?'

Logan was slow to answer. He was enjoying his revelations.

'I asked you because Doublejack is likely to be back in business in a very short time. He's out of detention, an' he should be headin' this way from Albuquerque right now. How does that news strike you?'

'That's great! Jest great! But will everybody be the same? I mean, well, sometimes a long spell in the penitentiary makes a man think twice before he goes raidin' again. I guess we won't know how Murphy feels until we see him, eh?'

'True enough, Jake. We won't know for sure until he gets here. But I'm thinkin' he'll take up where he left off, provided his confidence is strong at the start.'

Wagner frowned, making his features seem almost Asiatic. He stared at Logan, waiting for him to go on.

'I figure he needs a boost to put him on form again. Now, if one or two of his old cronies happened to pull a big job for him jest when he was startin' out again, I think that might make him forget about the inside of the pen an' anything else that was puttin' him off. Especially if what happened had a bearin' on something which had gone sour in the past.'

Wagner whistled quietly. He was reflecting that on all the other occasions he had sided Butch, the latter had never shown so much ability to think things out.

Logan resumed. 'Some years ago the outfit lost control of a sizeable quantity of loot. I've always been led to believe that the double-crosser was a fellow named Vargo, Gil Vargo.'

At this point, Logan shifted his posterior, interrupting his narrative. Some minutes earlier, a fly had alighted upon the face of Slim Petersen. His precarious position prevented his lashing out at it and thus giving away his presence. He did succeed in dislodging it, however, and the effort penetrated his consciousness sufficiently to make him aware of the resting men beneath him.

He listened, but did nothing to draw their attention to his position. Totally unaware that their conversation was overheard, Butch warmed to his subject.

'Yer, Gil Vargo. This Vargo fellow left the owl-hoot trail at a time when the outfit temporarily split up. He never resumed with his old buddies, either. Now, I happen to know that there's a thriving ranch not many miles from here, owned by the Vargo family.

'In recent years, it has doubled its size, an' I for one believe that the developin' came as a result of the Wild Bunch's loot, which Gil Vargo disappeared with.'

Wagner's brow was really corrugated by this time. He was at last beginning to guess at the line of action which Logan had in mind.

'I think I see what you are gettin' at, Butch. We could hang around and bump off this Gil Vargo, if he's still there. But that wouldn't really do Murphy any good. What he wants to get himself started up again is a little ready cash. The rancher will have his in the bank. We could rustle his cattle, of course, but that I've always found is a slow arduous way of getting rich. You have to become a cowhand in the process, an' I don't altogether see myself as a cow nurse.' He cleared his throat, closely watched by Logan, who had half a smile on his face. Wagner resumed. 'Of course, you might have thought of a scheme which doesn't occur to me.'

Logan waited a while, and then started to nod, very decidedly.

'I think there's a better way. It ain't the kind of strike I've ever made before, but I like the idea. I favour kidnap. By what I can hear the Vargo family is a closely knit one. Gil's brother, Raich, is the real rancher. He has a son, an only son. And that boy is the one we should

14

go after. Name of Dick. In his early twenties. If we had possession of that boy, I think we could touch his father for quite a few thousand dollars. What do you think?'

Wagner was interested; very much so. He was blinking more rapidly than usual, a sure sign that he was excited. 'It sounds like a worthwhile proposition, Butch, but I'd have to know more details. You'll allow I must be cautious at this stage.'

Butch nodded, satisfied for the time being. At the same time, a leaf and a tiny section of twig dropped on the hat brim of the tall man. A sixth sense seemed to tell Wagner that all was not well above him. Aware of the silence between them, Butch Logan looked him in the eye and saw that he was covertly looking upward, although his eyes were well back, under the brim.

Butch glowered and then glanced upwards. He started as he saw the outline of the man lying on the branch. His right hand went down to the Colt he favoured most and hauled it half way out of the holster. Wagner, however, dissuaded him. There were times when the flat, deadpan face could register definite messages.

Logan relaxed a little, contriving to look down. Wagner rose to his feet, said something about strolling over to his horse, and walked away without a backward glance. When he returned, a minute or more later, he had secreted under his arm a weapon which he scarcely ever used. It was an Indian tomahawk, which he had stolen from a homesteader who had given him shelter several years before.

Wagner came back and stood directly under the important branch. Without seeming to do so, he examined it. Then, quite leisurely, he gripped the handle of the tomahawk and aimed a blow above his head. His aim was accurate. The blade bit into a joint where a small branch forked out from a larger one. The lesser branch was severed.

It fell, and its severance was sufficient

to dislodge the man who had used it. With a brief cry of dismay, Slim Petersen fell earthwards, his head below the level of his feet. The back of his head connected with the earth, although he tried hard to cushion the blow.

Almost at once, his senses left him. He settled and remained in a tight, painful heap. By that time, Butch Logan was crouched over him with a gun in his right fist. A minute went by before the swarthy man believed that Slim was really unconscious.

He stepped back, perspiring a little and wondering at his buddy's sudden action. Jake fingered the blade of the tomahawk with his left hand.

He said: 'Doublejack would have approved of that, I guess.'

Logan grunted. 'To a man who once swung a double-bladed axe in a lumber crew a tomahawk would seem like a toothpick. But I go along with your meaning. What do we do with this hombre? He may have heard everything I said.'

Wagner bent down and examined the back of Petersen's skull. He straightened up, shaking his head. 'That bang on the head will have done him no good at all. I don't figure we need do anything about him. He'll have nightmares if he recovers. Let's move on.'

Logan allowed himself to be persuaded to leave without despatching the fallen man. Had he done so at that time, his action would have saved several determined outlaws a whole lot of anguish.

2

Slim had no idea how much time had passed by the time his head began to calm down and consciousness slowly returned. He was on his back with his head held slightly off the ground because it was infinitely more comfortable that way.

Every pulse gave a solid thump in the back of his head which left him slightly nauseated. He tried focussing on the branch up above and found that he could accomplish the simple exercise after a few tries. He felt his head rather gingerly and found that he had a sizeable lump on the back of it and a trace of blood which had matted his hair.

His hat lay a yard away. Would it fit, after what had happened to his head? He had his doubts. The hazy feeling in his brain was a new experience. He hoped it would pass. The shock of falling appeared to have soured his stomach, too, and that made things even worse.

This, obviously, was not one of his good days. He stood up rather cautiously, aware that his balance was not quite as good as he would have liked, and slowly collected his spurs, his gun and his hat. By tilting the old dun head piece well forward he found that he could wear it. Next, he went after the dun, and it was only when he was preparing to mount that his stunned brain went back to the remarkable conversation which he had inadvertently overheard.

Imagine a man reclining in a tree and hearing the beginnings of a kidnap plot! The whole thing was fantastic. But it was no nightmare conjured up by the beer he had drunk. He distinctly remembered the names of Butch and Jake, and an unusual name beginning with V — Vargo!

Gil Vargo, Raich Vargo and one Dick Vargo, who might become the victim of a kidnap plot. A family of well to do ranchers. Slim lurched up into the saddle and turned the dun about so that it would head back to town. He frowned at the thought of well off ranchers. In the past few years he had worked for several. Sooner or later, each and every one of them had somehow lost his respect. One or two had got started by rustling the cattle of their neighbours, and others had become rich by fulfilling army contracts which prevented them from going to war.

Slim felt that if only he could find a rancher who could hold his respect he would be able to settle in one place, and possibly improve himself. This far, after five years of wandering he had not succeeded, and working and wandering was begining to work out as the pattern of his life.

His thoughts now were far from his reasons for arriving in the district. He was thinking about outlaws and dishonesty and men getting on in the world in the wrong sort of ways. He felt a little disheartened and a slight increase in the throbbing of his head turned him back to his own immediate needs. He wanted a doctor, and he wanted him without delay.

★   ★   ★

Doctor Sam Scales, a veteran of the war between the North and the South, was paunchy and flushed. He had promised himself a very good living when he realised that he had survived the fighting of the 1860s and ever since then he had consumed good wine and food to excess.

His excesses in life, however, did not prevent his being the best medical man for many miles around Medicine Creek. After carefully bathing and dressing the contusion on the back of Slim's head, he regarded the patient through half closed eyes, with a hand across the lower part of his heavily-jowled face. Slim sat forward on the upright chair, feeling vulnerable and exposed.

'So that was how it happened, eh, son? You fell out of a tree while takin' a nap, an' you lit on your head, where it hurts?'

Slim nodded, quickly at first and then more slowly because that way his head did not hurt so much. He replied: 'I've told you once how it happened, Doc, don't try to make out I'm tellin' lies. What I'd like to hear is how to cope with the shiftin' cargoes in my head. Will all this pressure an' movement ease down, after a bit?'

'It'll go easier, no doubt,' Scales explained from his padded chair, 'but you'll have to be patient for a while, take things easy. You see, you're sufferin' from shock. Concussion, we call it. And that takes time to go right again. You'll know when things are right again, because the pain and the occasional dizziness will have left you.

'That'll be two bucks, if you can afford it, an' I'm sorry I can't do more for you now. You can call again later, if you're stayin' in town.'

Slim nodded and thanked him. He rose to his feet and cautiously slipped his hat into place. The pad which the doctor had contrived was not as big as the patient had at first feared. The hat went on, with a tilt. He paid the fee, explained that he did not know how long he would be in town, and left the building.

In the nearest eating house he ate two lightly poached eggs and felt grateful that his stomach would accept them. Shortly after that, he walked his horse by the bridle towards the saloon where he had taken the beer earlier. Outside the Painted Desert, he stopped and hitched the dun alongside of two other horses which were also awaiting their masters for similar reasons.

Slim had been thinking that a shot or two of whiskey might help his aching head. He sat down on the edge of the boards for a minute or two, hoping for some relief before he went into the badly ventilated building.

Quite by chance, his eyes lit upon the

brands stamped upon the other two waiting horses. The brand he saw was a big V inside a diamond. The sight of it started his memory working. His brain was clear enough, if only the fleeting pains would go. He looked the riding stock over. They were a palomino and a big roan, both in good lick and worth a lot of dollars.

A man with a clerical outfit and whiskey breath started to pass him by. Acting on impulse, Slim called to him. He turned, a few yards away, but did not deign to come closer. Obviously, he took Slim to be an ordinary drunk who had been ejected from the saloon.

'Mister, can you tell me anything about this brand, the Diamond V?'

After a brief pause. 'Certainly, it's the brand of the Vargo family who ranch to the north-east of town. Everyone in these parts knows that.'

The stranger moved on again before Slim had the chance to thank him. The young man's brain was busy. Some-where inside that saloon were two men who used Diamond V horses. Men from the Vargo ranch. Maybe this was an opportunity to pass on a timely warning about the kidnap plot. He felt his head and slightly sickened himself. He was in no shape to put the affairs of others before his own, but, seeing that he was intending to use the saloon himself, he would try to locate the Vargo men, if they didn't prove too elusive.

More lamps were lit than when he had been in before, and all the faces except those of the barmen appeared to be new ones. He made his way to the bar, and received a shot glass and a bottle. After two shots he thought his head was a little easier, but it was hard to tell.

He asked the barman who served him about the Vargos. The custodian of the bar tugged at his moustache, hurriedly glanced over the faces of the patrons and suggested that he should ask of the drinkers themselves. Assured that he was on the right track, Slim asked his questions.

26

No one acted really friendly. Two groups suggested that he should move on. A man in a third group stared pointedly at two men off in a corner, behind an unlit stove, and gradually Slim conceived the idea that the men in the corner were the ones he wanted to contact.

He lifted his hat as he confronted them, and smiled, glancing from one to the other. Each of them was young, in his twenties. They had the same harshness of basic expression and a way of weighing up a newcomer as if they were prepared for any sort of eventuality. A flash of insight told Slim that he had happened upon members of the family, rather than hired cowhands.

The one with the truly hostile green eyes had short-cropped hair and an unmistakable Roman nose. The other, who might have been a little older, had a Syrian rather than a Roman nose. Nevertheless, this feature was the dominating one in his face, as was the Roman protusion in the other. The second man had fair hair with reddish tints in it, not unlike the colour of Slim's own. He also had very steady green eyes and a flat-crowned stetson with a band of coins around it. A black leather vest masked the width of his shoulders.

'Gents, I have reason to believe that those two horses out there with the Diamond V brands on them belong to you. Am I right?'

The one with the grey eyes stayed silent, studying Slim's face without the slightest embarrassment. The redhead, however, could not restrain himself with the same ease. 'Look, buddy, if you're lookin' for work, we ain't interested. Is that clear enough? Now, take yourself off an' drink in some other part of the saloon. There's plenty of room.'

For the first time that day, Slim began to feel angry. He said: 'You sound like a hirer rather than a hired hand. Am I right in thinking that Vargo is your surname?'

There was an edge to his voice which did not go unnoticed by his listeners. The man with the grey eyes nodded slowly, as if without conviction. That was all Slim needed to invite himself to sit at their table. He pulled out a tall chair and occupied it. The redhead glared at him with eyes like gimlets, but he ignored the anger and made himself comfortable.

'I bet you boys are really well liked in this community. The way you turn on the charm sure must win you a lot of friends.'

He swished the remains of his drink around and tipped it down his throat. His head was throbbing, but not quite so badly as it had been out of doors. No one moved to have his glass filled, but he had not expected that. He began to explain his presence almost at once, knowing that he would fight shy of helping these arrogant young men, if they gave him any more superior talk.

'About an hour or so earlier, not far out of town, two hard-faced hombres were hatchin' a plot. They were plannin' to kidnap a young man named Dick Vargo, so as to take from his father, a rancher, a good deal of money.'

He paused having said this. Both faces across from him showed surprise and disbelief, but this time they obviously wanted to hear more. He obliged them.

'I was supposed to be asleep at the time, and I was not in a position to see faces, but the names of the men talking were Butch an' Jake. They meant business, all right, an' they said a whole lot more if I can only recall it.'

The redhead thumped the table with his clenched fist. 'Don't take any notice of him, Dick, he's some kind of nut. We ought to throw him out for havin' the nerve to come over here an' fake up a story like that!'

Dick looked from the redhead to Slim. He was reacting differently.

'Keep talkin', stranger. We have to hear more. If it's the truth you're talkin'

30

we'll know in a very short time now.'

'They talked about a man called Gil Vargo, who had once been an outlaw, an' how he had slipped away with a lot of loot. One of them thought the Diamond V had been built up with the stolen money. The idea behind the kidnap was that they should get back some of the money which belonged to them an' to an outlaw leader named Doublejack Murphy. How am I doin' on the truth stakes?'

Without having realised it, Slim had raised his voice since Dick issued the truth challenge. Several men drinking not far away had turned their heads in surprise. Nearer at hand, the redhead seemed transfixed by what he had heard. His face had paled and then flushed again.

Now, he pushed back his chair and rose to his feet with his fists clenched, his face and general attitude full of menace.

'Why, you scum,' he muttered through his teeth. 'Somebody has put you up to this to — get at me. All that stuff about Gil Vargo bein' a renegade an' all. I ought to shoot you here an' now!'

Slim, seeing he was about to be attacked, rose and kicked his chair out of the way. He noticed that the other Vargo was not in such a hurry to get to his feet, and this gave him a modicum of confidence as he danced clear of the cold stove and faced his adversary.

The redhead, who answered to Red, came at him at a crouching rush. One thing Slim was very clear about, with his head injury he was in no shape for a protracted fist fight. What he had to do had to be done quickly. He crouched himself, feinted with his left just before Red closed with him, and at the last possible moment, swung with a right.

The blow caught Red on the angle of the jaw and sent him backwards against the stove. Had it been heated he would have received a nasty injury. On this occasion, just as Slim's head was beginning to swim again, the stove merely checked the redhead's fall and helped to prod him into further action. Red started to advance again, this time watching more carefully and taking his time.

Slim blocked the first heavy blow with his left forearm. The second he took on his chest, moving away from it. He was gasping and feeling the room swim around him when Dick Vargo moved in from the side and held them apart. Red fought to get through to a man he felt sure he could lick, but Dick appeared to be the dominant character on this occasion, and the fighters stayed apart long enough for the action to fade a little.

Dick ordered Slim to desist. 'Break it up, mister. That's enough. You haven't done much harm, but some of the things you said hurt. Right now, I think you ought to go some place else. I believe you didn't mean mischief when you came in here. So thanks, and now, go.'

Slim nodded, and backed away. He

was thankful that Dick had interfered in such a timely fashion. His head was throbbing again. On the way to the bat-wings, he lifted his hat and felt over the sore patch. For the first time the Vargos and others noticed that he was hurt.

Mustering what dignity he could, he moved out into the street. He collected his horse, took it to a stable and left it there. Having asked about a hotel, he went and booked himself in, watched at times by many curious eyes. As soon as the key was in his hands, he retired to his room.

3

The tariff at the Creek Hotel was half a dollar to a dollar higher than in most hotels in the district. For the extra money, the stairs, corridors and bed-rooms had a decent strip of carpet down them, and the rooms which fronted on to the street boasted both curtains and muslin drapes.

The room in which Slim Petersen bedded down was on the hotel front. He was pleased with the two small mats, one either side of the single bed, and the chest of drawers, none of which were stuck when he tried to open them. Not that he had much to put in the drawers, or that he wanted to expand before turning in.

The pulsing in his head slowed him in his efforts to get off to sleep, but when he finally dropped off, lying on his side, away from the door, he really started to rest. Many hours had gone by; in fact the sun had gone down and the street was dark, before anything happened to disturb him.

Towards midnight, a tall thin man in trail garb ghosted along the boards of Main Street and paused in the dimly-lit foyer of the hotel, peering about him and listening, poised almost like an animal. After a wait of about two minutes, he seemed satisfied. He was about to dart up the stairs when he caught sight of the register, with its battered leather exterior.

Sheer curiosity made him tiptoe over to it and open it at the last page. He discovered that no less than eight rooms were occupied and three by single men. Two of them who occupied single rooms were well to do cattle buyers who gave their towns of origin as Kansas City and Amarillo. The third, in an unscholarly hand, had signed himself in as Slim Petersen, recently of Farwell, Texas. This was the resident the night visitor was interested in. He indulged in a grim smile as he read the sparse details and fingered the long article he carried in his left hand.

The room number and its location had been ascertained earlier in the day, but the tall man took pleasure in knowing that he could have found out all the necessary details for himself without any trouble. He closed the book again, carefully replaced it in the same position in which he had found it, and went quietly up the stairs two at a time.

The room he sought was about five yards along the front upper corridor. As he stood before it and peered up and down at the rooms on either side, he held the long-handled weapon in his left hand quite tightly. It was attached to his left wrist by a thong, but he discarded it, thong and all, and laid it on the carpet while he prepared to enter the room.

The door was locked, and to make things a little more difficult the occupant had left the key in the lock.

Fortunately, the intruder had plenty of patience and he did not lack confidence. He took from his pocket a small home-made tool and went down on one knee.

Even working in the dim light of a turned down corridor lamp, he managed to turn the key into the required position in two minutes. The critical time followed. The occupant, he knew, had taken on liquor before retiring, but the injury to his head might have prevented him from sleeping deeply. Any slight noise might disturb him, and then what had to be done would have to be accomplished with a slight element of risk. The tall man thought about the risk and then frowned. By the way of a change, he yawned. He was impatient now of delay. He felt supremely confident that if there was any hue and cry he would be out of the building long before the sleepers could rouse themselves sufficiently to see who had caused the trouble.

He deliberately pushed the key so

that it fell out of the door on the inside and tinkled on the floor. For a few seconds, the intruder waited, listening with an ear quite close to the panels, waiting for an indication that the sleeper within had woken up. None came.

He tried the door again. The handle turned easily. The door was no longer locked. He picked up the weapon which he had deposited on the carpet and slowly moved through the door opening. As soon as he was inside, a slight movement at the window showed that he had let in a light breeze. A drape was fluttering. He closed the door behind him and regarded the outline of the sleeping man a few feet away from him.

The weapon was in his hands as he studied the sleeping figure. Once before on this day, he had used it against this sleeping man, and the fellow had had a painful accident. He had not been hurt badly enough to put him out of action. Subsequent events, and some loud talk in a saloon showed that this fellow was a menace. He had to be eliminated.

The intruder stepped up to the bed. He stopped a foot away and then inched closer. He was studying the angle at which his victim was lying, under the blanket. His aim was to bury the narrow blade of his weapon in the sleeping man's neck. A single blow, or possibly two, would be sufficient to cause death. He perceived that the sleeper had his back to him. He would be striking from over the right shoulder.

The tall man stepped back one pace and did a couple of practice downward swings. He moved back again, and raised his right hand with the handle of the weapon held firmly in it. His downward swing towards the body was half completed when the sleeper betrayed for the first time that he was not in a deep sleep.

The shoulders of the resting man were braced, and the body moved away, over the edge of the bed just as the blade of the weapon bit into the bedding. The assailant gave a deep gasp of surprise. At the same time, the intended victim slid down on the far side of the bed, reaching out with one hand for the gun belt which he had hung over the bed head.

In clawing after it, he knocked the belt to the floor. While the intruder was slowly recovering from his initial surprise, the survivor — Slim Petersen — kicked himself clear of the blanket and got the holster between his two hands. He was expecting his attacker to leap over the bed and spring upon him, but this did not happen.

In the few seconds of brief respite, Slim had the Colt in his fist. His teeth were clenched as he rolled away from the bed and strained his eyes for the first glimpse of his assailant, who, for the moment, was out of sight. If he was not following up his initial attack, perhaps he would retreat through the door, his point of entry.

Slim had heard the key fall to the floor without its significance registering properly. He knew now, that the brief sound it had made had probably saved his life. But he was not yet safe . . .

He peered under the bed, looking for the feet of his assailant. The bed cover, however, was trailing low and it was not possible to tell at a glance where the fellow was. In actual fact, he was straining to tug the bladed weapon out of the bedding, but the blade was so firmly embedded that he had to haul really hard.

Suddenly the blade came away and the attacker lost his balance and fell backwards. His weapon shot out of his hand and hit the wall. Slim was startled into firing without pausing for a proper aim. He missed by a couple of feet, because the attacker went away from the door, rather than towards it.

Slim ducked again, expecting retaliatory fire, but none came. Instead, the tall man headed straight for the nearest window and pulled aside the main curtains. His outline, even then, was shadowy. He jumped, and for a second or two it was not clear as to which way he had moved.

Slim hesitated before firing again. The sudden crash of breaking glass took him by surprise. The figure had seemed to shrink and then jump towards the front wall. Clearly, he had chosen the window as the quickest exit, but he had taken quite a chance in going through it in the way he did.

His jump left quite a sizeable hole, and the secondary drapes went with him. Slim moved slowly to his feet and cautiously approached the window. By the time he arrived there, the daring leaper was just somersaulting off the front ledge of the hotel awning, on his way to the street below.

There was a thud as the body landed, and the muted sounds of a man breathing hard. Footsteps sounded, moving up the boards towards the west end of town. And then a brief silence. The silence seemed to give confidence to many people who had been intentionally keeping quiet. Shouts came from either end of the street. First one man, and then another, moved about in the hotel. A woman gave a querulous cry, which was half hysterical.

The man with the grey walrus whiskers who came to Slim's door in a quilted dressing gown turned out to be the manager.

'Is — is everything all right in there? What's goin' on?'

'It's all right to come in, if you want to see for yourself,' Slim assured him. 'I've had an intruder, but he's left now. Come on in. I'll turn the lamp up.'

He had already put a match to the hanging lamp, but now he made it brighter. Heskett, the manager, came in, looked around and was shocked at first by the hole in the window. Slim gave him a few clues as to what had happened.

The manager's relief was obvious. It overwhelmed and took the place of his anger. He sank down on the bed, feeling far less uncertain of himself, and went so far as to offer his client a small cigar. Slim accepted it gratefully, and struck a match for both of them.

A female receptionist holding a small hand gun appeared at the door, but the manager shooed her away to pacify the noisy protesting clients in other parts of the building. Down below, in the street, a few men had gathered.

One of them was the town marshal, who shouted up to know some details. Slim and Heskett crossed to the window, and the former began the explanation.

'My name is Petersen, marshal. This is my room. Some hombre broke in a short time ago and tried to kill me with a long bladed weapon. As you can see, he failed an' he came out again through the window. If it's of any interest, he ran off towards the west end of town.'

'All right, Petersen, go back to bed now. I'll see you about a statement in the morning. Right now, I'll jest see if there's any sign of your prowler.'

The marshal pushed his way through the crowd and walked off in a westerly direction. Some of the curiosity mongers started to leave almost at once, but before Slim could withdraw from the window, a voice which was vaguely familiar called up to him.

'Hey, Petersen, this is Dick Vargo. Would it be all right for me to come up there an' talk to you for a few minutes?'

Slim sniffed. His first inclination was to deny the privilege, but he could not deny his continued interest in the Vargo family, and he felt that he would like to talk to somebody about the latest happening.

'It's a kind of funny hour for visitin', Mr. Vargo,' he grumbled.

Red Vargo chuckled rather grimly. 'Don't make out you're goin' straight off to sleep after what's happened, mister.'

Slim recollected only too clearly the anger which Red had shown earlier in the day, but he did not for a moment anticipate more trouble with these two young men. He glanced at the manager to see if he had any objection to late night visitors. Heskett threw up his arms, leaving the matter entirely in his hands.

'All right, then, come on up, but don't make a noise on account of other folk!'

Slim ushered Heskett to the door, assured him that the draught coming through the broken window would not seriously interfere with his sleep for the rest of the night and showed him out. He was lying on his side on the bed, sucking contentedly at the cigar when Dick knocked on the door and entered, just ahead of his cousin, Red.

Red seemed slightly self-conscious. He was probably thinking back to the fist fight of the afternoon. Dick, however, prowled the room and soon discovered the tomahawk which had so nearly ended Slim's life. He came back with it and tried it in the hole in the bedding, and found that it fitted well. Dick held up the weapon, and bestowed upon Slim a glance of enquiry.

'That almost certainly severed a tree branch this afternoon and let me down with a bump when I heard that talk I told you about. The same man who caused my earlier accident obviously came back here tonight to finish me off.'

Dick sat down on the foot of the bed, his hat pushed back. 'Did you have any enemies in this area, before today?'

'None that I know of, friend. This attack must have had something to do with my revelations in the saloon. Someone overheard them, and this is the result. If you weren't convinced then, perhaps you are now. There's trouble afoot for you, not of my makin'.'

'I'm convinced, Slim,' Dick admitted readily enough. 'If we didn't seem particularly cordial towards you, I regret that, too.' He glanced across at Red, who was leaning against the chest of drawers. Red cleared his throat and nodded very decidedly, approving Dick's deliberations.

'Perhaps we can make things up to you a little,' Red suggested.

Slim eased his head a little higher, and glanced from one to the other without enthusiasm. He thought that they were considering giving him a reward of money. Because of his particular attitude to ranch families, that would have been a mistake. But he had guessed wrongly.

Dick explained: 'We propose to stay here until daybreak and make sure that no further attacks are made upon your person tonight.'

Slim relaxed, and even grinned. 'Oh, well if that's what you have in mind, by all means make yourselves at home. Spread yourselves out.'

While he tucked himself in, and prepared for sleep again they did just that, appropriating spare blankets and making themselves as comfortable as possible quite close to the door and the window. They withdrew, as they had said they would, at daybreak.

He did not hear them go.

4

In a similar room to the one occupied by Slim, Dick and Red Vargo lounged on their twin single beds, smoking and moving restlessly around the time when other townsfolk were beginning to emerge from their houses and walk the streets. Their hotel was towards the other end of the main street.

'Whatever you may think, Dick,' Red was saying, 'somebody's out for your blood, and you ain't been back from the army for more than a week or so. There are times when it seems to me that the Vargo family is always goin' to be dogged by trouble.'

Dick shifted his position and propped his head on the other arm. 'It could have been worse for us, Red. After all, your Pa never went to the penitentiary although it was pretty clear to a lot of folks that he had been ridin' the owlhoot trail.'

50

'Yer, yer, I know. He should have paid for his sins like the other raiders, but he didn't. Not that it did him a lot of good. He was never happy on that smallholding your Pa gave him. He was too restless. And Ma couldn't stand the way folks looked at her, them knowin' Pa wasn't all that he should be. Pa was weak, I guess. It was the war between the North and South which unsettled Gil Vargo. He was never the same man after it.

'Ma died before her time of a broken heart, an' Pa died last year without makin' anything of himself in spite of him managin' to stay out of jail. Me, I've been stuck with that old maid aunt, my mother's sister, an' that ain't been more than passin' comfortable, either. There's been times when I've wished she'd stayed on the other side of the Rio Grande, so help me, I have!'

In his disturbed state, Red found it hard to stay on his bed. Before Dick could answer, or pacify him in anyway, the redhead leapt to his feet and started to pace the floor in his stockinged feet. He was sucking furiously on a cigarette. Dick knew that he had something to ask, and he thought he knew what it was; but he waited.

Red paused, first in front of one window and then at the other. He glanced at Dick, and away again. At length, he moved to the foot of his own bed, and asked rather uneasily: 'Dick, will you tell me truthfully what do you think about the question of that loot?'

'You mean about whether the loot was ever used to build up the Diamond V?'

Dick Vargo rubbed his long Syrian nose and peered at his cousin through half-closed eyes. Red nodded briefly.

'Your father was always cagey about that loot. He never even admitted that it was anywhere near the Diamond V. An' since he died, my Pa has been jest as quiet about it. My Pa, however, always maintained that he built up the spread with his own brains an' money. 'Shrewd buyin' an' sellin',' he always said.

'Me, I've always believed him. He's a good businessman. He never felt the need for any illicit capital. In fact, he never borrowed from anybody, other than the bank. So why don't you stop tormentin' yourself on that score, an' let's talk about other things.'

Dick sounded brusque, rather than persuasive, and yet Red knew that they had to discuss other things, now that Slim Petersen had bulldozed his way into their lives. And yet, even then, Red was not quite ready to face the latest problems. He gestured nervously with his right hand.

'Since you came back, my thoughts keep returnin' to those unhappy times, three years ago an' more. And why you went away, to divert suspicion an' anger away from me.'

'If it'll make you feel better, talk about that first,' Dick suggested. He was showing a great deal of patience.

'I was wild, in those days, Dick, real wild. I'd admit it to you like I wouldn't admit it to anyone else. That girl, Lily

Legrange, I really took to her. She had a way of makin' a man do risky things jest to hear her gasp an' see her smile. She was passin' pretty, too, with all that long brown hair and those mockin' green eyes.

'Her Pa, Walter Legrange, he acted like he didn't like havin' me around that homestead south of town. He had a powerful voice, Walter had, and he used it on me when I'd been out ridin' with Lily one time when he didn't know about it. So, after that, I always kept my distance. He always referred to me as 'that darned fool young Vargo.'

'I guess I was in love with Lily, an' I would have done anything for her. Anyways, after a bit of schemin' to keep her Pa out of the picture, she got so that she could slip away now an' again an' meet me by the creek. That was when the canoein' started.

'At first, it was great fun. We both enjoyed it. It was like bein' in a new world, a place built only for two people. But Lily was not easy to keep satisfied.

She had to have bigger an' better thrills, an' that was what drove me to take the canoe across to that other stream, the one with the down stretch on it.'

Red paused for a moment, dry-mouthed.

'You mean the rapids,' Dick prompted.

Red nodded. 'Yer, the rapids.' He stopped talking for a few moments, and all that time his eyes were flashing as though he were reliving the past. 'That canoe was not true. I mean it had a slight tendency to slew away, off the line you wanted it on. That didn't help. I did my best to keep Lily happy on the safe part of the stream, but she had these sudden bouts of great excitement, you know.

'An' she insisted on paddlin' herself. Maybe you know as well as I do that two folks paddlin' have to be used to one another. They have to work as a team. If one of them does something the other doesn't expect then they're both in trouble. Canoes are the easiest boats I know to turn over.'

Red was seated on the end of his bed by this time, with the fingers of his two hands locked together.

'When I tried to get us into the side on the excuse that she ought to take a rest, she suddenly started to paddle against me, an' that meant we had to go further on. There was a lot of laughin' an' good natured arguin' at the time, an' before I knew rightly what was happening, we were hearin' that muted roar that always comes up from the rapids.

'I shouted a warnin' to her. She was sittin' up front in the boat, an' she didn't seem to hear. Jest once as the current got a hold of us, she turned her head right around and her eyes were round with fear. I see those eyes at nights, all sort of compellin' an' green an' haunted in their depths.

'You've heard the story of my troubles before, so you know there ain't a lot more to tell. Well, she panicked. I did what I could an' we sailed through a few hazards, then Lily started to paddle for dear life. First one side an' then the other, as one gnarled rock after another rushed nearer in the racin' waters.

'She missed one or two, nearly exhaustin' herself in the process, an' then a couple of big ones came up close and she used up all her remainin' energies in tryin' to fend them off. As a result, we clouted one of them almost broadside, sheared the hull on the other and finally capsized jest beyond in a deep pool of dark creamin' water that looked as if it was boilin'.'

Red sucked in breath, and seemed as if he could not go on. Dick waited for a while, and then took up the story. 'Poor Lily was sucked down in the pool and washed right away. All that was ever found of her was a large brimmed picture hat with a pink ribbon in it.

'You had a couple of cracked ribs, an' after you got home again you ran a fever for the rest of that week. Legrange started to look for his daughter, but nobody could find her. A whole lot of folks joined in the search, on foot an' on horseback.

'After a time, they pieced a few things together. Somebody found the wreck of the canoe, an' there was something in it which pointed to Lily's Vargo beau. So Legrange came a-lookin' to the Diamond V, after first callin' on the law in town. But my Pa got wind of the visit, an' he thought you deserved a break, after the sort of life your Pa had led at one time.

'Pa knew I was restless, that I wanted to go away from the spread, not jest settle down on it an' take over gradual control. So we had ourselves a talk, and we came up with the idea that we should allow the local folks to think that *I* was the one who had been keepin' company with Lily. An' I took off in a hurry, as though I was broken hearted, and joined up with army cavalry. Until a few days ago. Now I'm back, so where does that leave us?

'Most of the folks in these parts have ceased to feel deeply about poor Lily's death. Legrange an' those at his house, of course, will harbour a grudge for all time, but that can't be helped. And now somebody wants to kidnap Dick Vargo, me, all on account of some old family skeleton.'

Dick rubbed out his cigarette, crossed to the window and yawned. Red threw himself backwards on the bed again. He was still tensed up and a prey to his own emotions.

'It was a big thing you did, that time, Dick, goin' off into the army to draw suspicion away from me. In fact it was too big a thing, goin' away for three years. I shan't feel at ease with myself unless you give me a chance to do you a big favour in return. I know how the account could be squared between us. You want to hear about it?'

Dick was prepared to argue that black was white, but nevertheless he answered with a positive nod.

'These jaspers who are plannin' to kidnap you. They must be around here, some place. If you got back to the home buildings of the ranch, kidnap would be jest about impossible. Too many men about. So maybe they intend to jump you before you get back there. But there's two of us here, so why don't I pretend I'm you? Maybe the kidnappers don't know either of us all that well. I could act as a decoy, have them jump me instead of you. That way, you'd have it easy to make your way back home. You certainly deserve a peaceful spell at home after bein' away three years. What do you say?'

Dick clicked his tongue in disgust. 'I appreciate you might feel indebted to me, Red, but the feelin' will wear off. Try to forget about it. As for actin' as a decoy, the whole idea is ridiculous. One Vargo heir is as good as another. When they found out you were not me, they'd try to raise the money on you, an' because you'd deceived them they'd be tougher with you than with me.'

'If they realised I wasn't the heir to the ranch, they'd grow tired in time of tryin' to get money out of your Pa.

Maybe they'd beat me, but they'd let me go. I still think it's an idea worth tryin'.'

Dick's brows suddenly shot up. He ironed out the expression on his rather broad face, and slowly shook his head. He was thinking that if the kidnappers realised that they had the son of former outlaw Gil Vargo in their clutches they might give him a thoroughly bad time and then kill him.

He said: 'No Red, drop the idea. It's right out of the question. I don't want to hear about decoys any more. As far as I'm concerned you don't owe me a thing.'

A few minutes later, the cousins went out into the street. They ate a hearty breakfast, and partook of a haircut and a shave, but all the time they were busy Red was withdrawn into himself. He had always been prone to morose moods, so Dick did not pay any particular attention to him. It was not at all clear what Red was thinking about.

Almost an hour later, they returned

to the room they shared and started to talk about moving out. Dick packed his few loose articles rather quickly. He was checking through the drawers when Red struck him from behind and robbed him of his senses. The blow was struck with a pistol barrel. Red had waited until Dick put his stetson on, so as not to harm his skull over much.

As soon as Dick was unconscious, Red hauled him across the room and dumped him in the bottom of a tall wide wall cupboard. The redhead was breathing hard as he trussed and gagged his cousin with short thongs and a spare green bandanna.

Presently, Red straightened up again. He had changed his appearance in order to make himself look more like Dick. Now, he had on Dick's distinctive black leather vest, his flat-crowned black stetson with the band of coins around it. He hoped his slight change of expression would help to fool anyone who found it hard to tell them apart.

After making sure that Dick would

not suffocate in the wall cupboard, he left him there and went down below, taking his belongings with him. He engaged the attention of the veteran clerk at the desk, paid the bill for both of them and intimated that 'Red' had already left the building and would not be back.

The haircut each had taken at the barber's had been a close one. Close enough to fool a casual observer into thinking that his red hair was really fair with reddish tints in it. After leaving the building, he hurried to the livery and there he called for Dick's beautifully built palomino.

The ostler did not query his choice of horse. This was partly because of the shadow in the building, and partly because his sight was past its best. The palomino knew Red, and did not complain when he finished rigging the saddle and blanket and finally mounted up. Red's own roan, stalled further away, whinnied in protest when it was left behind.

Fifteen minutes later, Slim Petersen, looking very much better for his rest, found his way into the hotel where the cousins had stayed and enquired about them at the desk.

'I'm sorry, sir, you're jest too late,' he was told. 'Mr. Dick came down in something of a hurry about a quarter of an hour ago, an' checked out. His cousin had already left. There's no forwardin' address, but I take it you know the Diamond V cattle ranch is well within a day's ridin' distance, if the matter was urgent.'

Slim took off his hat and ran his fingers through his hair. His battered head felt a whole lot better; the pain was almost gone. Now, however, he was disappointed. He was in no way clear as to how important it was to have contacted the cousins before they left town.

'I don't figure it matters all that much, mister,' he called back, as he was going out of the door.

On the way up the sidewalk, he was shaking his head and looking baffled.

5

After collecting the palomino, Red gathered confidence. He had started to act a part and did not intend to spoil it by hiding himself on the way out of town. He figured that in doing what he was his cousin, Dick, would be paid out for past favours.

Half way along the street, he paused while the palomino drank out of a stone trough. A little further along, he dismounted and bought the makings in a mercantile store. In yet another shop he bought a box of bullets, and finally he called across the street to a man who was a mere acquaintance.

'Hey, mister, did you happen to see my cousin, Red, leave town?'

The man questioned gravely shook his head.

Red shrugged. 'Oh, well, I guess it don't matter really. We're headed

Cottonwood Springs way, an' I guess Red will have taken the longer route through Indian Gulch. It sure is a whole lot better for a ridin' man who has the extra time. I'll be goin' that way myself, if he happens to turn up lookin' for me. Adios, amigo.'

The acquaintance soberly touched his hat as Red rode away. He was wondering why there should be a sudden interest in him, where before there had been indifference.

Red had been riding for an hour when his troubled mind came up with something Dick had happened upon when they were still together. If it became known to the outlaws that he — Red — was the son of the man they wanted to get even with, Gil Vargo, they might try for the reward and then kill him instead of letting him go.

He began to wonder if he had not done a particularly foolhardy thing when he took upon himself to masquerade as his cousin. Kidnap, in itself, was a scarifying thing, but tangling with his father's sworn enemies was even worse.

Unconsciously, he began to push the palomino to a better pace. He thought back to the brief conversation he had had with Dick about this jaunt. All he had offered to do was to act as a decoy. How would it be if he stuck to that? Just a decoy, a man to take the kidnappers out of their way without offering them a victim.

He wondered if he was sufficiently smart to pull off such an action. He knew the route he was riding. That helped a little. A great deal would depend upon how many men were likely to pull the snatch. Slim Petersen had given the impression that there were two, but they might have brought other outlaws into the business, as well.

If anything, at this stage, his senses were too acute. He was seeing signs of hidden men in every bush, behind every upthrust knob of rock. Forcing himself to be calmer, he reined in under an outcrop of rock and looped a leg round his saddle horn.

All that talk about taking the Indian Gulch route had been to put his would-be captors in the right route. They could scarcely have left town ahead of him. If they were not to work the snatch from behind, there was only one course open to them. They would have to hurry out of town by the more direct route to Cottonwood and make a hurried change from one track to the other over faintly marked animal tracks and anything else they could find.

One thing Red was sure of. There was at least one possible way of getting through the morass between the trails on horseback, and anyone knowing the way could get through to Indian Gulch in reasonably quick time. He felt that if they knew their business, and if they planned to take the chance he had deliberately given them, they should get ahead of him without too much difficulty.

Since his more recent thinking, however, such a consideration did not leave him feeling at ease.

The stagecoach and general wheeled vehicle route between Medicine Creek and Cottonwood was old, broad and rocky. Not very much vegetation grew close to the trail to break up the harsh landscape for the traveller. Because of that, very many horseback travellers took the Indian Gulch loop because it was relatively lush with trailside vegetation and it gave shelter and a certain amount of shade.

Red began to think ahead. He found that he did not know the route in as much detail as he had thought. His tortured imagination began to play him up, so that he lost a lot of energy in perspiration. That which ran down his face left a salty taste in the corners of his mouth.

He wondered fleetingly if cousin Dick would have been freed from his uncomfortable position in the hotel wall cupboard, and what had happened to the unfortunate cowpuncher, Slim Petersen, who had clashed twice in one day with the kidnappers.

Presently, while his thoughts were still ranging wildly over many unpleasant possibilities, he topped a slight rise and felt the change in grade as the palomino started down the other side. Fleeting memories came back to him. This gentle downgrade lasted for quite a long way. On either side, trees and sturdy scrub grew quite close, masking the terrain beyond.

One other serious geographical development had a bearing upon the immediate future. Wide of the trail, and hidden by the timber on either side, were two converging hogsbacks which came steadily closer all the way down the slope until near the bottom, where the track was reduced to a narrow defile, not wide enough to accommodate two horses passing.

Thus far, Red's foreknowledge carried him. The most obvious place to be attacked was the narrowest. He felt that he had perhaps a quarter of an hour in hand, and possibly half a mile in distance.

Directly ahead of him on the downgrade there were still many trees of the scrub oak and pine variety. For a time, at a slower pace, he registered some little comfort from their presence, thinking that only when the timber gave out his troubles would start. But he was not able to relax for long. The very narrowness of that defile would make it almost impossible to slip through unmolested.

He would almost certainly be made a prisoner near that spot, unless the palomino galloped him clear, or some minor miracle occurred.

He was seeing the narrow spot so clearly in his mind's eye that he almost missed another sinister movement very much nearer. Some twenty feet up a tree which overhung the narrow track there were signs of a heavy intruder. This was no wildcat, but a two-legged human up to no good. As soon as he had divined this, Red became a little calmer.

He was forewarned. The spot was

fifty yards ahead of him still. What should he do? Someone was preparing to drop on him from above, or, alternatively, drop a loop on him. He had to avoid passing under the tree. That was obvious.

If this was a kidnapper, he would probably drop a lariat loop. Falling on a man from that height might break his neck, and a corpse might not prove a particularly good bargaining instrument in a kidnap case. Red deliberately enlivened the palomino's pace. When the distance to the tree was halved, he suddenly swerved to the left and went right away from the tree in question with his body held low over the horse's weaving neck.

He thought he heard a frustrated cry, but he could not be sure. He had about fifty feet to manoeuvre in before he swerved again behind rocks of medium height close under the edge of the hogsback on that side.

His senses were alert, and his hopes were building. If that had been the planned attack, perhaps he might — after all — get through the narrow gap unscathed. Twenty yards further on, when he was considering putting his mount nearer the beaten track, two revolver shots came whining after him from the tree in question.

Both bullets missed him by more than a yard, but he had been thoroughly startled. He had just made up his mind that guns would not be used, so that he could be captured unharmed, and now his theory was being proved wrong. Why the bullets? he wondered. And could he expect more to be aimed at him?

Where was the other man, or other men?

His mouth dried out very considerably, as he tried to work out afresh his enemies' strategy. He swung the palomino first one way and then the other, but no further shots occurred. His spine was crawling with apprehension as he tried to work out how much further before the twin hogsbacks brought a crisis in his life.

Fifty yards? more than fifty, or less
. . . Swaying foliage made it difficult to
estimate. He was licking his dry lips
when the unexpected happened. A taut
lariat appeared right ahead of them, a
perfect trip-wire skilfully hidden. Red
cursed. He tried to force the palomino
to leap over it, but the horse and man
were far too close.

The animal tried to negotiate the
obstacle, but it failed. Its forelegs were
whipped from under it. It sprawled
sideways, falling, and took Red with it.
Rather belatedly, he tried to get his
boots out of the stirrups, but he was
unlucky. One came out without any
effort, but the other stuck.

Only when his body was hurtling
earthwards did the second foot slip
clear, and thus give him a sporting
chance as he hit the ground. He tried to
land on all fours, but the falling horse
jostled him, knocking him sideways. His
right shoulder hit the ground with a
jarring thud which shook his teeth.

Red's flat hat flew off his head, and the

black leather vest, not long out of the shop, lost a goodly portion of its surface. It would never look quite as good again. Red's body skimmed hurtfully along the ground until his freshly-cropped skull connected with a low firm rock eroded from the trail surface.

His senses never left him, but a shocking wave of pain passed through his skull and made him shudder. He had a vague notion that the palomino was scrambling to its feet again, and then he was closing his eyes in an effort to minimise the pain.

*   *   *

Butch Logan's well filled black shirt was faded through constant washing. Only where he had perspired did it appear to be retaining its original colour. Shortly after Red had crashed to the ground, Butch, the nearest outlaw, stood in the shade of a tree casually rolling the last two inches of a cigar around his rather full, red lips.

Having tired of the cigar, he blew it out of his lips and watch it somersault through the air, to land in a clump of bunch grass, still trailing smoke. Leisurely, he walked across to it and thoroughly rubbed it out with his boot. Next, he tramped across to the ambush spot and carefully undid his lariat. He was thinking that Jake Wagner was his friend, and a fine old buddy. At the same time, Jake was not as thorough as he might have been in a two-man team.

Jake had allowed the eavesdropper to stay alive in the hotel in Medicine Creek, and now he had failed to stop this Vargo with a loop dropped out of a tree. Butch figured that old Jake was not as efficient as he had been before the last Wild Bunch had split up. Within certain limits, however, Logan was a tolerant man. He thought that with a bit of practice, in the right company (his own) Jake might still be a formidable fellow when honest men were around to be rooked.

Slinging the lariat over his shoulder, Logan slurred his way to where the fallen man lay. His right hand crept into his fist and he assured himself that Vargo had lost his weapon when he made contact with the ground.

Logan glanced briefly at the victim. He smiled to himself and went in search of the dislodged hat. He brought it back and stood over Red just as the latter started to stir. The fallen man screwed up his eyes and glared at him.

Logan said: 'Howdy, Mr. Vargo. You sure did come a cropper jest now. You must have done that head of yours a whole lot of no-good! Here's your hat. If you aim to be as careless as that again when you're ridin' I'd advise you to push your hat on a little tighter. It might protect you a bit.'

Red spat out and raised himself on an elbow.

He started to say: 'How do — ' and checked himself. He had meant to ask how this fellow knew he had the right man, but that would be a foolish question as this stage.

Logan hooted with pleasure, his

77

thick-set figure shaking, and his pock-marked face oozing perspiration.

'How did I know who you were? Well, that ain't too difficult. I was told to look out for a man with a big nose an' a sort of frosty domineerin' look on his face. Hair fair to sandy coloured, an' sittin' a fine palomino hoss. An' you fit the description, as well as in one or two other details, Mr. Vargo. So the time is ripe for us to get acquainted.

'In jest a minute or two I'd like to introduce you to a ridin' companion of mine. He's a little further up the hill but he won't be long.'

Logan glanced up the slope. While he did so, Red peered around him to try and locate his missing gun. When he looked up he found that Logan had been watching him the whole of the time out of the corners of his eyes. Moreover, the threatening gun moved as if it had life of its own.

Red found himself shuddering inwardly.

6

Ninety minutes after his first incarceration in the wall cupboard, Dick Vargo was free again. He was, however, feeling very much the worse for wear, and when an aged room maid burst into the bedroom, intent upon straightening the beds and preparing for another visitor, he was stretched out on his bed, ruefully feeling his wrists and ankles.

The woman pulled up short, just inside the door. Her face looked anguished. She applied a hand to her wrinkled skin and started to explain.

'You — you must be one of the Vargo gents. But I was clearly told that the pair of you had left. Your — the other gentleman paid the bill and said the room was empty. I don't rightly know what to do now. Do I take it that you are movin' back again?'

Dick glared at her, unintentionally.

He shook his head rather vigorously. 'No, nothin' like that. It's true we're supposed to have moved out. I, er, I came back for something an' as it took me a long time to find it I'm still here. Give me five minutes more, an' I'll be gone.'

The woman withdrew, apparently satisfied. Dick waited until the door was closed before pulling out his cigars and selecting one for a smoke. He was still angry, and, as he was one of those people who anger slowly and then remain in a rather unpredictable state for a long time, the immediate future augured badly for anyone who crossed him.

The double doors of the wall cupboard were secured at floor level by a catch which slotted downwards into the floor. He had bruised his shoulder before he managed to spring the catch and thus give himself access to the room proper. More time than he had thought was wasted in getting out of the cupboard. After that, it was only a matter of minutes before he had his hands on a knife and was able to free himself.

He felt a bit sick about the latest development. Red had the Vargo wilfulness to a marked degree. Now, he had gone off with the intention of posing as the Vargo who ought to be kidnapped. He had put himself into a whole lot of trouble and danger, and, what was so baffling, it was difficult to know just how to go about helping him.

Dick waited until he had smoked the whole of his cigar. When he was satisfied, he tossed the butt of it down into the dirt of the street. His gathering together of property took no time at all. Downstairs in the foyer, the efficient desk clerk called out to him.

'Oh, Mr. Vargo. I surely thought you'd left about an hour or so ago. Your cousin checked out an' said as much. Ain't no harm done, but since then a young fellow came askin' for you. A tall young man with a freckled face, an' sort of medicated pad on the back of his head. He wasn't unlike yourself for hair colourin' — '

Dick interrupted. 'Thank you, I think

I know the man you mean. What did you tell him?' He walked a yard or two nearer the desk.

'Well, like I said, I thought you'd checked out, so I recommended that he got in touch with you through the ranch, the Diamond V. Was it all right to tell him that?'

'Certainly, it was the only thing you could do. Adios.'

The clerk returned the farewell greeting. Dick left the building and walked along the boards with his gear slung over his shoulder. Red's hat, now gracing his head, was the same size but a slightly different shape to his own. In addition, he was missing the dark leather vest which had never been off his person in daytime since he came out of army uniform.

The situation had an air of total unreality. Dick did not know whether to dash out of town; nor did he know where to dash to. He could scarcely go along to the peace office and say that his cousin was on the point of being kidnapped somewhere. It wouldn't have sounded right.

His only useful contact in the town was the cow-puncher, Slim Petersen. A hurried visit to the other hotel made it clear that Slim had also left the town, with no intimation as to where he was going.

After fretting over the situation for a short while longer, Dick took time out to drink a couple of beers. It was as well that he did so. In the saloon was a fellow who had been around when Red left town. Dick learned where Red was headed for, and by which route. Ten minutes after that, he was mounted up on Red's big-boned roan and heading out of town in the direction of Cotton-wood.

★　★　★

Dick also had interesting and worth-while views upon the best kidnap spots on the loop route to Cottonwood, but as he was not in the kidnapper's confidence, he felt that he could not risk setting off up the short, direct route and then cut across onto the Indian Gulch trail.

So he followed up the action in the tracks of his cousin. His sign reading was good. He was so thorough that his progress was slow. He had stopped twice for brief halts on account of thirst when he noticed the area on the track where Red had diverged to avoid the tree ambush. The time was around one in the afternoon. Instead of going off to one side and searching out the detour, Dick kept straight on, at an even slower pace. Just when he was beginning to think he had made a mistake, he noticed the tracks of one horse coming in from the lush grass back onto the trail.

At that point, he dismounted and took a closer look at the sign for the next few yards. He had learned a lot about tracking from army scouts, and now his knowledge was standing him in good stead. He decided that when the palomino came back to the track that it was moving at a rather faster rate.

Something had panicked Red higher up the grade. He wondered what it was. Had someone fired at him? Or had he merely noticed something which he wished to avoid? Maybe time would tell. Horse and man had most certainly moved along in this direction, and perhaps they were still further ahead and unmolested. Dick discounted his own theory as soon as it occurred to him.

He had come to believe in the information which Slim Petersen had made known to them. He felt that there was a kidnap in the offing, and that cousin Red was in a very vulnerable position. A few yards further on again, still short of the narrowest part, he came to a halt, whistling quietly to himself.

A further perusal of the track from a kneeling position suggested that the palomino had been brought down. Red had been unhorsed. At first he thought that the pale horse had been wounded, but reason, after a time, made him think otherwise. He guessed the truth, that it had been tripped. His first concern was that the animal had not seriously injured itself in any way. Almost at once, he felt a slight feeling of guilt. Red was the one he ought to have been really feeling for. How had he fared when the long-legged high-stepping horse had been knocked from under him?

Conjecture took him nowhere. All he could be certain of was that Red had been attacked. The kidnap had been carried out. The wrong cousin was in the hands of men who hoped to make a fortune out of him. After rocking his saddle, Dick mounted up and pushed on again. He soon became aware of the extra sign left by other horses.

Now, his attention was diverted by the terrain which lay ahead. He had come through the defile, and the down slope was gradually levelling out and widening. Presently, the trees and fern began to fall behind and the rougher, rockier type of landscape which made the other trail so plain crept in from the east.

Stretching out towards the north and west was a series of small undulating hills and valleys. Withered grass grew in the valleys and sage and mesquite clothed the higher levels. Neither near nor far was there any sign of man. It was an arid, isolated expanse which old timers in the area vaguely associated with ancient mines.

Dick glared at it from under the borrowed hat brim. This wilderness had swallowed up his cousin, as well as the men who had kidnapped him. He thought that perhaps a wilderness was a good place in which to keep a kidnapped man. In any case, kidnappers would not want to move their victim around very much, so soon after the snatch. Their next move was to get in touch with the person expected to pay out.

Someone had to get himself along to

the Diamond V. While that person was away, Red Vargo had to be held, rather than toted about. So he had to be somewhere in this wilderness; within a few miles, one way or the other. Dick had little to encourage him beyond his own deductions, but he had made up his mind to stay in the area and await developments.

In the middle of the afternoon, Slim Petersen, having failed to contact the Vargos in town, was approaching a lush valley due south of Medicine Creek. He was coming to the end of the long ride to see the folks who had raised him after an absence of five years.

★ ★ ★

In the last half hour he had ridden around the foothills which hid the valley and the creek from anyone approaching it from the north. He had ridden past an old broken down trestle bridge, and now he was sending his dun through the shallow waters of the creek ford, on his way to the Legrange homestead, which was the first of several stretching out in a westerly direction.

When he left, five years ago, the buildings had amounted to no more than a log house and one barn. Now, he saw before him no less than five buildings, all scattered rather hapazardly over an area amounting to half an acre.

Pop Legrange certainly had made progress in the last five years. Twinges of conscience began to ruffle Slim as he looked down at the distant scene of moderate prosperity. How had he managed to stay away for the whole of that long time?

He went back into his memory, trying to work it all out. In his first year away, when he was in his nineteenth year, he had assisted on two long cattle drives, one of them as far as Wyoming. He recollected that he had felt violently homesick on one or two occasions during the Wyoming drive. After that, he supposed, the business of being away from his foster parents had not bothered him so much.

Now, rather belatedly, he thought that he had neglected his folks.

Pop Legrange had been a fit and able man of fifty-two when Slim came away. He had looked as if he would live for ever. Legrange was a rotund, barrel-chested man with silver hair cropped close round a sunburnt bald spot on the crown of his head. His rather full body had always been supported by a broad belt. Slim had always said it was a wrestler's belt, and in the long warm evenings of summer Pop had wrestled with the boy in a good-natured fashion, as though to prove it.

Pop's wife, an ailing woman about ten years his junior, had died a few years before Slim left. Her death, however, did not much affect the ménage, because the two girls, Lily, Pop's daughter, and Maria, an adopted child, had been old enough to take on a lot of the womanly chores in Mrs.

Legrange's failing years.

As the dun splashed out of the shallows, Slim wondered how they would be faring. He made calculations to bring himself up to date. After a short pause, he decided that Pop would now be fifty-seven years, his daughter, Lily, twenty, and Maria Tomkins, just a few months younger.

He wondered what sort of reception he would get, after such a long period away. Would he have been forgotten by the others, or would they remember him with affection? In a way, it was a pity he had never formed the habit of writing letters. His homecoming might be a shock to them, for, after all, he had given them no reason to believe he was still alive.

Barring his way into the surroundings of the house was a five-barred gate, one which had been replaced since he left. If his mount had been fresh, he would have hauled off and leapt the animal over it, but a wealth of experience in and around cattle ranches made him forego that youthful pleasure on this occasion.

A dozen or more young chickens were pecking the ground inside the fence. He was weighing them up for size when a bright female face appeared at one of the kitchen windows. His arrival had been noticed. Scarcely was he through the gate than a slight familiar figure in denims and a man's patched shirt came tearing out of the back door in mocassins, wiping soap suds off her arms on a worn towel.

'Slim! Slim, how nice to see you!'

The young girl who had come to meet him was about three or four inches over five foot in height. She had a nicely rounded figure under the masking masculine garb. Her long black hair, which was a foot in length, came away from a centre parting and was held back at the nape of her neck in a blue ribbon.

The wide-set radiant eyes which so enthralled the new arrival were violet in colour and very attractive.

The girl halted a few feet away, out of breath, with her breast heaving. 'Oh, Slim why in the world didn't you let us know you were coming?'

Slim shrugged away a sudden feeling of bashfulness. 'Why, Maria, would it have made a lot of difference to the reception?'

The smile flickered off the girl's face, and then reappeared. She stood below with her hands on her hips, regarding him closely. 'No, Slim, I guess it wouldn't have made all that difference, after all.'

Slim thought he detected a note of sadness in Maria's voice. This far he had been enthralled with the change in her appearance. When he had last seen her, she had been leggy, almost like a young boy. Now, she had filled out in the obvious female places, as he had always expected she would.

In the back of his mind, he was groping for the old image of Lily, so that he could compare the two. A little game, long remembered, brought them a little closer, while he was thinking. Maria came closer, reached up for a stirrup and swung up behind him on the dun's back.

At the same time, Slim glanced across two meadows, and saw in the distance the familiar rotund figure of Walter Legrange. Pop was behind a plough, half way down a furrow which ended two hundred yards away. He was coming towards the house, coaxing good labour out of two veteran shaft horses. His powerful shoulders were brown. His shirt was elsewhere, along with his hat.

Slim waved and at once received an answering wave, as though the old homesteader had recognized him at once. Maria pushed her body against him and gave him a sensation which was a trifle on the new side. Maria Tomkin had been taken in by the Legranges when she was less than ten. She and Slim were the adopted ones. They had always been very fond of each other.

Slim said over his shoulder: 'It's good to see you again, Maria. An' you've changed, but I suppose all girls of your age do that.'

Maria chuckled as he sent the doubly-loaded dun around the other side of the house. Slim was watchful. His eyes were scanning the curtains of the house as they made the circuit. He also took in the nearest of the two barns and the cow shed. After a brief pause, when no conversation took place between them, Maria had a sudden flash of intuition. She knew what he was thinking.

'Oh, poor Slim. You can't have known. It's hard to think that you've been away so long. Ain't nobody here to make you welcome exceptin' Pop an' me. Lily ain't with us any more. You sure you didn't know that?'

Slim reached around behind him and carefully lowered Maria to the ground. Somehow, she contrived to hold onto his hand until he dismounted himself. He shook his head and held her close while she prepared to break the sad news to him. Already, he had an inkling that there was tragedy to be talked about.

'Lily died, Slim, about three years ago. She was drowned in a boating accident with — with a young man. Things have been pretty lonely around here since then. But I don't want to make you feel sad right at the outset of your homecomin'.'

There was such a look of appeal in the violet eyes that Slim held her to him. The dun eyed them from a few feet away, totally unnoticed. They were still in the same position when the homesteader's powerful voice roared out towards them from the other side of the house.

'Where in tarnation is that stay-away boy of mine puttin' himself I'd like to know?'

Only then did the young couple's embrace relax. They stood a little way apart, waiting for their foster father to appear.

7

All through the main course of the substantial meal which consisted of young beef, potatoes and two green vegetables, Slim was glancing across the oval table, either at Maria, who made occasional trips to the kitchen, or at old Pop, to see if his appetite was in any way impaired.

And all the time that he was eating avidly, he was weighing up the possible effect of Lily's tragic loss on the man who had expended so much energy and affection upon his foster children and his ailing wife.

The room was devoid of any photographs of the dead. Out of doors, there was clear evidence that a great deal of honest toil had gone into the soil. Pop had several acres under cultivation, and he had a small herd of cattle on the hoof, too. But what had the death of his daughter done to him?

Walter put on a bold face during the meal, wisecracking about the government in Washington, about the price that beef was fetching in the southern states and how little Medicine Creek changed on his infrequent visits to town.

Towards the end of the meal, Legrange made a remark which showed he had almost divined Slim's thoughts. 'If you're trying to work out who's changed the most, I can tell you right away. It's little Maria, there. She works twelve hours a day, every day, an' she never wilts. Ain't that something? By the way, you ain't rightly said this far, Slim, how long you are plannin' on stayin'?'

Slim sat back on his chair. The question had baffled him. He could see that there was plenty of work around the homestead for an active young man, but when he had planned the visit, it had been more to see how the old folks were getting along. He had expected to see one or other of the young women married, with her man about the place. He was still not recovered from the shock of knowing that Lily was dead, and that little Maria was doing all the women's work on her own.

'Pop, will you give me till tomorrow to answer that question? I'm happy to be here, but I didn't know how things would be until I arrived an' there's things I want to think out for myself before I come to any decision about my stay. So give me time to work things out, will you?'

Legrange nodded very decidely, but he averted his eyes. He was disappointed, but he did not want to show it. He was thinking that it should not take a young man long to decide that he wanted to stay home for a while, particularly when he had had five years in which to get rid of his restlessness and maybe sow his wild oats.

'Take all the time you need to come to a decision,' he suggested mildly. 'Meantime, you two young folks need to get better acquainted. For this night, an' this night only, I'm goin' to wash up the dishes so that Maria can go out ridin' with you. So, when you've smoked a cigarette, Slim, I'd count it as a favour if you'd run out the ridin' mare.'

Slim offered to help Walter with the dishes before the two of them went out riding. He also asked Walter to ride out with them, but the older man replied firmly in the negative to both suggestions. He knew Maria needed youthful company when the chance came along, and he also knew that she had things to tell Slim which would have been more difficult coming from Walter himself.

Consequently, Slim and Maria were setting off down the bank of the placid creek which irrigated the land in Nester Valley and made it such a desirable spot for farming people to settle in. For a time, they rode close, Slim on the dun and Maria on a sturdy black mare.

The girl's hair was spilling out like a shining black bell now, unhampered by the ribbon. It was contrasted with the light flat-crowned stetson which sat her head rather squarely.

Slim glanced towards the surface of the creek waters, with low flying insects skimming its surface. 'Can you remember the days when we used to slip off down there and bathe in our underclothes?'

Maria arched her brows and smiled. 'It ain't quite the same when there's nobody to go in the creek with you.'

Slim thought he ought to cheer her up. 'I can confess to you now that we're both grown up, there were times when I went a little further down, on my own, and bathed naked.'

At this revelation, Maria laughed out loud. 'I can tell you now that I crept along there when you were bathing alone an' took a long look from under the trees! And what's more, I often bathe that way myself these days. Ain't nobody around to take account of any more, so it doesn't matter.'

Suddenly they were both laughing,

and recounting little incidents from the past. After a time, Slim reined in and glanced across at his companion. 'I don't figure you'd care to take a bathe right now, would you?'

Maria blushed becomingly. 'Well, not right now, Slim, although I could be persuaded if a fellow asked me another day. Tell you what I would like to do, though. I'd like to swim the horses across the creek and take them down to Half Mile Rock at a gentle pace. Then we can dismount, an' I'll roll you a smoke, like I used to do when you were jest learnin' how to cope with tobacco for the first time.'

Slim thought of one or two occasions when he had almost made himself sick through smoking tobacco which was much too strong for him. Maria did not wait for him to come back to the present. She dismounted, slackened her saddle and sent the mare plunging into the water.

Slim put the dun into the water a minute later. He called: 'Your boots will shrink up on you, Maria!'

She turned in the saddle and waved her hat at him. 'Oh, no, I won't. I've had them wet before. They've done all the shrinkin' they're goin' to do, mister!'

Slim pushed the dun after that, but he did not overtake the mare, which had had a lot of practice in creek swimming. Up on the other bank, Maria suggested a race to the distant rock. Slim agreed. He gave fifty yards start and he was only just overhauling her when the rock pinnacle flashed by, jutting into the creek.

The beaten young man was slightly disgruntled. He dismounted rather hurriedly and pointed an accusing finger at the girl. 'I thought you said we'd go down to Half Mile Rock at a gentle pace?'

Maria pushed her hat forward and wagged her finger in return. 'That was before you'd agreed to my horse race challenge! An' now, find me a nice place to sit down. I want to relax in your company. Did you bring your Bull Durham with you?'

Slim nodded. He handed over his tobacco sack and went in search of a comfortable place in which to sit. Two minutes later, he found the sort of place he sought. It was a natural seat, the back of which was a fallen log. They were able to sit up against it with their legs at a lower level, just over the water.

'How will this do?' the sandy haired young man asked.

Maria nodded and smiled. She rolled a smoke with dexterous fingers and applied it to his lips. He was immensely aware of the closeness of her as she leaned over to apply the match. While he drew on the smoke, she flopped against him, so that his shoulder bent up her hat brim.

'There's a special question I have to ask you, Slim. It's the sort of thing that a woman would have to ask. May I ask it now?'

Slim's freckled face showed his perplexity. He had no sort of inkling what it was she might want to know. 'Ask away,' he suggested airily, 'anything you want to know is okay by me, I guess. After all, we were raised almost as brother an' sister.'

The violet eyes became intent upon his own. He blinked, wondering what sort of a spell she was hoping to put him under.

'Slim, you got an almighty shock when you heard that Lily was dead. Were you by any chance in love with her while you were away? I mean, was she the main reason you came back home this time?'

Slim turned away from her, drawing on his smoke to gain time, and absently fingering his sideburns which would soon require a trim. Why, he wondered, had Maria asked this question of all questions? He was a little naive as to her motive. Her eyes were so intensely upon his own that he answered frankly and honestly, not at once seeing the reason for her apparent anxiety.

'I loved her, I guess, like all of us did.

After all, she was that sort of a girl, always full of fun, as though she was tryin' to make up for the miserable times we all knew due to her mother's illness. But it wouldn't be true to say I came back specially to see Lily. I came back to see everyone. Does that answer your question, Maria?'

She blinked her eyelids a couple of times, very slowly. 'Yes, that answers my question,' she replied softly, 'but it doesn't necessarily give me a whole lot of satisfaction.'

Slim leaned forward and stared at her. She was pouting a little and he thought it made her look rather pretty. He had kissed a few girls on his travels and now he thought mischievously that he would steal a kiss from Maria.

He took her face in his hand and, after a momentary hesitation during which she studied his eyes with the old intentness, she went along with his wishes, melting into his arms and matching his efforts with her own.

Slim was breathless when they came

apart. He glanced at the girl and saw that she had derived some satisfaction from the kiss, and yet, at the same time, he did not think that she was wholly pleased about it. He did not know sufficient about womanly wiles to know why, so he changed the subject. He sensed a certain coolness in her attitude as the matter of fact tone came back to his voice.

'Maria, there are other things I have to know. About Lily's accidental death, and maybe other things. I can't ask Pop about them because it would be too painful for him. So I'll have to ask you. There's no one else I can turn to.'

Maria did not answer. She appeared to be staring intently at a small insect in the grass. Slim, however, could feel the beat of her heart against his side.

Without knowing quite why, he prefaced his remarks by saying: 'I'm glad you're not married.'

Emotion surged through the girl. She leaned forward and put her arms round his neck. 'What was that you said, you old stick in the mud?'

'I, er, I don't rightly know . . . why I said it.'

Slim floundered around, but the kiss which Maria started had something extra compared with the first one. Eventually, she backed off a little with a glint of satisfaction in her eyes.

'Maria, was she with a man when the canoe accident occurred? Did you say it was a canoe, or some other sort of boat?'

'I didn't say, but it was a canoe. They were over on the other stretch of water, the one with the rapids in it. How they came to be over there I'll never know, but I can't think the man was altogether to blame. You see, she became passin' wilful in the years when you were away. She was never satisfied with anything for very long. Anyways, that little jaunt was the end of our poor sister. They never found her body.'

Slim groaned. 'What, what happened to the man? Was he punished in any way?'

'It all depends what you call punishment, I'd say,' Maria opined disconsolately.

'*Who* was he, Maria. You ain't said his name, surely it was known. Was it anyone *I* knew?'

'It wasn't a name a person could easily forget, Slim. Vargo. Dick Vargo. Son of a family over towards the north-east of Medicine Creek. Well to do ranchers.'

Without being aware of it, Slim clenched his hands on Maria's arms. She must have been immediately aware of the shock he had received.

'*Vargo?* Are you sure the name was Vargo? Dick Vargo?'

'There was never any doubt the name was Vargo, Slim, but why do you ask like that? What are the Vargos to you? Do you know them?'

'Sure,' Slim admitted slowly. It had become apparent that he had a slight head injury when he took off his hat for the meal. Now, Maria began to suspect that the head injury was something more than a fall out of a tree.

'Did the Vargos have anything to do with that cut on your head?'

'Yes, but only in a roundabout way. Now, are you sure it was Dick Vargo who was out in the boat when Lily lost her life?'

Maria studied his face again before answering positively. 'Yes. Dick Vargo. Pop went over to the Vargo place when the local peace officer found something by the wrecked boat which suggested the Vargos. Raich Vargo, he's the rancher, made out it was his son, Dick. He also said Dick was very cut up about the accident, so much so that he had gone off an' joined the army to try an' forget what happened to Lily.

'Pop explained that Dick goin' off into the army wouldn't give him his daughter back, but Mr. Vargo reasoned with him, and he calmed down after a time. After all, it was an accident. And the rancher gave Pop a hundred dollars to order a head stone for the burial ground in town. You can always go back there and take a look at it, if you want to, but Pop has another little place at the back of the house where he has his own memorial tablet.'

Slim said: 'I've got news for you, Maria. Dick Vargo is back from the army. I've met him, and his cousin, Red. But if anyone had asked me to guess which of the Vargo boys had been in that accident with Lily I'd have said it was Red, not Dick.'

Maria gasped and moved onto her knees. 'Strange you should say that, Slim. I've always had the same impression. Lily always kept her beau well away from Pop's scathing tongue, but she gave me a clue or two before that fateful day as to who he was, and I could have sworn she said once it was Red. But how could we both be mistaken? It had to be Dick, didn't it?'

'I'm not at all sure, Maria,' Slim admitted, as he slowly clambered to his feet. 'One thing I do know, though, I shan't rest straight in my bed till I've contacted the Vargos again. I won't have to stay long. Maybe I'll ride out tomorrow, in the middle of the morning.'

As he grabbed Maria's leg to boost her into the saddle, he noticed that she was shivering. 'Have you caught a chill or something, sis?' he asked, in the old familiar way.

She shook her head and did not answer until she was ready to ride away. 'Tell me, if you go lookin' for the Vargo boys, will it be for purposes of revenge?'

Slim frowned. 'I don't rightly know that there's anything which wants avengin', Maria. As a matter of fact the Vargos have trouble without me goin' along after them to shoot the livin' daylights out of one of them. I need to make contact again to see how they're makin' out, as well as seekin' the answer to this puzzle you've set me. This business of who was involved, Dick or Red.'

When Slim denied outright vengeance, Maria experienced some sort of relief, but it wasn't much for a young and pretty woman whose hopes had been suddenly raised by a young man's reappearance. All she could be sure about was that he was leaving again after one solitary night under the same roof.

8

At three in the afternoon, two days after the kidnap, a stocky somewhat over-dressed man in his early forties was riding on a buckboard pulled by a roan and a bay. The vehicle was on a lightly marked track north of Medicine Creek and west of the far-reaching Diamond V cattle ranch.

The man's name was Dixie Malone. He had a closely-trimmed black beard and moustache, and a derby hat which had soaked up a deal of perspiration in the twelve months he had been wearing it. Malone was a travelling barber and dentist. His teeth were brown, and he had little trouble with them, but the same could not be said of his cranial hair.

His beard and moustache were frequently trimmed, but the hair on his head was only touched about once every two months. Consequently, it always appeared to be sprouting down the back of his neck, and its general appearance would not have led his customers to believe that haircutting was his greatest skill.

Fortunately for him, however, many people out in the country preferred the attentions of a travelling barber rather than face a trip into town to a barber's shop. Because of this, Malone continued to prosper, even after fifteen years during which he always seemed to tell the same jokes to his customers.

The bearded man was headed for the Diamond V. Raich Vargo was expecting him. The rancher always laid on a haircut for his men. He paid for it as an extra to their wages, and the visit of Malone passed a carefree hour or so.

On this particular occasion, Malone's visit was likely to be a slightly different affair. Just how different, he had no idea, of course. What he did know was that a stranger had given him a small parcel to deliver to the owner of the ranch. A golden eagle had changed hands before the stranger went on his way, and now the perimeter of the Diamond V was alongside of him, which meant that he might be on the outside of a cooling drink within the half hour.

As it was, the roan and the bay made good time over the remaining distance, and the home buildings of the ranch rose into view after twenty minutes. Malone, who liked to cut a dash on occasion, then called for their best speed and sent them up to the paddock gate in a whirling cloud of dust.

The blacksmith and an old handy-man coughed and grumbled before they saw who it was arriving like a charioteer.

'Glory be,' exclaimed the old handy-man, blowing out his cheeks, 'if it ain't old Dixie Malone all araring to be cuttin' hair! That'll be the day when he makes a couple of bucks out of me!'

The old man, whose head was almost completely bald, always trimmed his own beard. On this occasion, he threw back his head and laughed at his own words. The blacksmith, who looked upon a barber's shave and a haircut as something of a luxury, hurried forward to open the gate, and warmly shook the visitor by the hand as he sent the vehicle through, on its way to the open space in front of the house.

Raich Vargo was up on the gallery with his legs stretched out and the flaps of his khaki shirt outside for coolness. The owner of the ranch was fifty-two. He had a shock of white curly hair, a grey moustache of imposing proportions and straight black brows. In the last ten years he had put on extra weight and that made him look shorter in the body than he really was. He was massaging his ample paunch through his shirt as he studied the alert face of the visitor.

'Well, Malone, I don't hear you rattlin' a pocketful of other people's teeth, but you look happy enough in your work. How is life treatin' you?'

Dixie grinned, showing his brown teeth. He nodded towards his host. 'I can see that I arrived jest in time to give you your seasonal hair trim. Got a little surprise for you this trip, as well. How about havin' your hair fixed first this afternoon? The boys in the bunkhouse can wait a while. I have my reason, Mr. Vargo.'

The rancher thought it all over in a matter of a couple of minutes and agreed to be the first to go under the towel. A Mexican serving woman came from the rear of the house bringing coffee for the new arrival. While he was drinking it, a few items of saddlery were moved out of the way on the gallery, and the master's best upright chair put in place for the operation.

Vargo stood up, while the servant tucked the towel in around his collar. His eyes were on the conveyance which had just arrived. His handyman was bringing water for the horses. As soon as that was done, the same man ran a duster over the rear of the vehicle, paying particular attention to a heavy, padded arm chair, with a head rest, which was fixed down to the base of the buckboard, facing towards the tail.

This chair served its purpose both for the extraction of teeth and for the cutting of hair. Most of Raich Vargo's men were keen to sit in it; but not so their boss. Raich was clearing his throat almost before Malone had finished his coffee. He beamed at the travelling man, taking the edge off his impatience.

'Since you arrived, Dixie, I've found myself gettin' real keen to have that haircut.' He yawned rather noisily and sat himself down in the high chair. 'I meant to ask you something before you started. Have you seen my son on your travels?'

Dixie surrendered his empty cup and slipped off his soiled frockcoat. Resplendent in his double breasted waistcoat, he waited, his tools to hand. A look of surprise was spreading across his hirsute countenance.

'Dick? You mean Dick is back from

the army? No, I can't say that I've seen him around, Mr. Vargo. Where is he supposed to be stayin' since he came home?'

Dixie pushed back his derby, and seemed extremely keen to hear the reply. He learned that Dick might be almost anywhere, seeing as how he was taking a few days off to get himself acclimatised again before settling down to serious work.

Mr. Vargo folded his arms under the towel, and set his face in a frown. He was concerned about Dick's continued absence, and Dixie, moving closely around his head, knew enough of the look in his eyes to realise this. He wondered why the rancher should be concerned about a capable young man like his son, an energetic young fellow in his prime with a useful army background.

He tried out one or two jokes on the rancher, and only received a lukewarm response. And then it occurred to him what he ought to be doing to put the client in a better frame of mind.

'Doggone it,' he remarked, in his lively fashion, 'I've got a small parcel for you, an' I almost forgot. Hang on a minute, I'll get it out of my coat.'

Dixie dropped it in the rancher's lap, on top of the towel. Vargo said for him to take a breather while he opened it and found out what it was all about. Dixie was quick to back off and to roll himself a thin smoke. He lit it and sucked on it with his back resting against a supporting post.

Presently, the rancher whistled. A thin, emaciated face appeared at the window of the nearest room. Nell Vargo, the rancher's wife, had been suffering from a rheumatic type of illness for several years. These days she was confined to a wheelchair or her bed, and mostly she stayed in the parlour, occasionally looking out.

Raich assured her that he did not want anything. He then gave his full attention to the contents of the parcel. There were only two items. A message, carefully written in ink, in sloping writing, and a man's finger ring. The ring was in gold, with the Diamond V cattle brand prominently displayed on the top.

Vargo fingered the ring, while he read the startling message, over and over again.

To Raich Vargo.

Your son Dick has been kidnapped by men who have no reason to like the Vargos. If you ever want to see him alive again keep your own counsel and act as follows.

Insert a message in the county seat newspaper saying that $20,000 will be paid for the Bonanza, then wait to be contacted. Just that and no more.

★　★　★

'Is it bad news, Mr. Vargo?' Malone asked carefully.

'Let's say it comes as a surprise,' Vargo replied, after a pause. 'I want you to think very carefully about the fellow

122

who gave you this parcel and tell me exactly what he looks like. Had you ever seen him before?'

'Never in my born days,' Dixie answered fervently. His eyes focussed into the middle distance, and his tongue moistened his lips while he was thinking. 'He was a tall fellow with kind of dead lookin' eyes an' no brows to speak of. Sort of flat featured, an' there was something a bit different about his hat, but I can't remember what that was. Any special reason why you have to know, Mr. Vargo?'

Vargo sniffed and put the message and the ring away from him, in the wrappings. 'Finish me off quickly, I want to think about something special, Dixie. Come on now, get a move on.'

The barber's fingers were rippling constantly as he hurried through what remained of the haircut. He knew that he was the carrier of bad news, but he was not sufficiently close to the rancher to insist on knowing what it was.

The job was almost finished when a

single rider covered in dust came off the Medicine Creek trail and walked a jaded dun up to the ranch house rails.

Slim Petersen touched his hat, and gestured for permission to dismount. The man under the towel seemed to be trying to ignore him, and the barber did not want to encourage him in any way.

Slim said: 'Good day. I think I may be addressin' Mr. Raich Vargo. I can see I've come at an awkward time, but my business has to do with the family. Can you possibly tell me if either of the boys is on the premises?'

The rancher turned his head sharply, and narrowly missed getting the tip of the scissors in his ear. 'The boys?' he repeated sharply.

Slim crooked his leg round the saddle horn. 'That's right. Either Dick or Red would do. I can assure you that we have met before. I was talkin' with them jest a few days ago in Medicine Creek.'

'In that case, I'd be glad if you'd get down off that cayuse an' step inside to talk to me,' Vargo suggested curtly.

The rancher gave one hard glance at the barber, who promptly gave up the haircut and withdrew the towel, dusting his client down and murmuring about how he was going into the bunkhouse right away to get on with the job in hand.

Indoors, Vargo pointed a sharp finger at the gaunt figure of his wife, in the chair by the window. She managed a ghost of a smile for Slim's benefit and promptly withdrew into herself, watching him as though there was something quaint about him.

Slim was embarrassed by her at first, but the rancher's brows were beetling and he had to keep his attention in the owner's direction.

'Neither Dick nor Red is anywhere around at the moment. Now, I'd like to ask you who you are, an' what the nature of your business was with the Vargo boys in Medicine Creek.'

Slim put his hat under the upright chair which he was sitting on. He flexed his fingers as he thought over all the happenings since that afternoon in the tree. 'I'll be glad to tell you, Mr. Vargo, but I'd better tell you to hang on to your chair because you may be in for one or two shocks.'

Slim said who he was and where his last job of work had been carried out. He then launched into a narrative of the events connected with the planned kidnap, and the attack upon his person in the hotel bedroom.

He finished up by saying: 'I've been payin' a visit to Nester Valley since I left Medicine Creek, but I wanted to make sure if the boys had got back here because I really an' truly felt that one of them was under a serious threat. I'll be frank with you. Their continued absence makes me fear the worst for them. Have you had any sort of word from them yourself?'

Vargo took a deep breath. He handed over the document brought by the barber with a hand which trembled a little. 'This arrived jest a short while before you did. Read it. No one else knows it has arrived, except for the barber and he doesn't know the contents.'

Slim took the paper with a sense of foreboding.

What he read upon it did not make him feel any better. 'They've run into trouble,' he remarked unnecessarily. 'That is to say, one of them has. Dick, according to the wording.'

Vargo nodded. He was toying with the ring. When Slim raised his brows, the metal band was passed over for his inspection. He examined the device upon it with great interest and then turned it over, glancing at the inside of the ring.

'Hm, this has a big R on the inside. I suppose it does belong to Dick. I'd have taken the R to stand for Red. But then I'm not family, an' could make a mistake.'

Raich Vargo was startled by this revelation. He was absolutely certain in his own mind that his son and nephew had never in the past swopped their identical rings. He was convinced that this ring had been taken from the hand of Red, and he said as much.

Slim smiled rather grimly. 'In that case, they've snatched Red instead of Dick. But where is Dick?'

Vargo's mouth quirked into the ghost of a smile. 'If I know my son, he'll be hangin' around somewhere close waitin' for a chance to spring Red loose. We Vargos, we like to keep our own house in order. It's a matter of pride.'

Slim asked a few questions which were answered. Everything appeared to have gone over the head of Mrs. Vargo, for which he was pleased. No woman could take the shock of knowing her son had been kidnapped — not easily, anyway.

'Slim, I said jest now we keep our own house in order. This seems to be an occasion when we need a little outside help. You've been in on this kidnap thing from the beginning. How would you like to act as my representative in this dirty business? You could do the insert in the newspaper, an' carry out the kidnappers' instructions for me. I could give you a letter, signed by me, which would give you authority to act in my name. Now, what do you say?'

Slim nodded. 'I'll do it, Mr. Vargo. In the circumstances, I wouldn't be much of a man to turn down the chance to help. But it's likely to be a very tricky business, an' you do well to trust me on such short acquaintance. I think Dick would have approved, though.

'I'll do as you say, an' if I get started without delay I could take a look around an' see if I can come up with anything. After all, I have a couple of painful old scores to settle with this outlaw mob, myself. I'm sure you would approve, if they could be thwarted before we have to part with your money.'

'I would,' Vargo assured him warmly, 'but it's the boys I'm bothered about. You haven't shown any surprise that I'm goin' through with this business, even though in fact they've snatched the wrong man.'

'I did notice, Mr. Vargo,' Slim said, 'an' it says a lot for the ties of blood in your family. I hope I don't let you down.'

The rancher gave him a long look of appraisal as he moved away to the desk to write out a letter of authority.

9

The sun had set and risen again by the time that outlaw Jake Wagner re-entered the hilly wilderness between Medicine Creek and Cottonwood Springs. At ten in the morning the tall renegade was feeling pleased with himself. He knew that Butch Logan's opinion of him since they joined forces again was not very high, but in his handling of the ransom note, Jake thought that he had done a good job and that Butch would surely have to think better of him.

On a high spot, west of the place where he had parted company with his partner, Wagner stopped the progress of the dusty black stallion and mopped himself with a bright bandanna. To boost his morale he did a couple of practice draws with his pair of nicely balanced .44 Colts. He thought that the return of Doublejack Murphy to the

131

field of raiding and highjacking would give him, Wagner, all the confidence he needed to return to his former reputation as a man to be avoided.

He yawned, thought that things might be a whole lot worse, and felt around the area of his saddle scabbard. Alongside of the rifle nestling there was a second sheath, the one where he normally kept the tomahawk. He was disappointed about that, about his having left it in the Medicine Creek hotel. There was a limit to the ways in which a man could use a tomahawk, but he liked it, and he had looked upon it in the past as a good luck charm.

After a few moments' rest, he shrugged off his feeling of disappointment and started across the minor hills and valleys to the rendezvous. All the time he was moving across, he acted warily, avoiding the highest grades and keeping to the hollows wherever possible. This kind of going took more out of the stallion than did the slightly more even terrain further east.

Fifty yards short of the hollow Wagner was heading for a curt voice called: 'Hold it right there!'

Although Jake recognised the clipped tones at once, he nevertheless flinched. His dead pan eyes were searching the low crest ahead of him for the man who had issued the challenge. The black had stopped of its own accord. It rolled its neck at its master, but did not share his surprise when Logan casually rose to his feet on their left flank.

Logan chuckled wickedly. 'Hell an' tarnation, you sure did look scared, Jake! Are you sure you weren't followed?'

Wagner shook with a brief anger. 'Shucks, Butch, you have the darnedest way of irritatin' a man! Why did you have to do that? Of course I wasn't followed. So calm down, will you, an' show a bit of interest in my return!'

For a minute or two, Logan ignored the new arrival, moving round the rim of the hollow and studying the terrain over which his partner had arrived. His spy glass told him nothing that he did not want to know about. With his gun slung under his arm, Logan slouched down the hollow and walked up the other side with Wagner and the black beside him.

The next hollow was a wide one. It had the shape of a Mexican steeple hat, except that the steeple itself was low. There was a ring of stunted trees around its crest, and the hideout was cut into it. The dugout's front wall faced east, but it had a short tunnel going out through the west wall, providing a useful bolt hole for anyone needing to get out in a hurry.

Red Vargo was reclining uneasily on a narrow shelf cut into the earth wall on one side and shored up with short timbers. His wrists were tied, and a further thong hobbled his ankles. He glanced quickly from one man to the other as they came in, ducking their heads.

Logan shot the prisoner an unfriendly glance. He had a feeling that Vargo's anxiety would be increased if Jake and he did their talking in front of him. Wagner looked as though he would have preferred to exchange information without being overheard.

The two outlaws sat down on either side of the table, and Logan went to work with a tobacco sack.

'Well, Jake, so you delivered the message. How did you make contact? Did you tie the note to an arrow an' aim it at the buildings from a distance?'

Wagner shook his head very decidedly. Belatedly he grinned at Logan's attempt to amuse. 'No, I didn't do anything like that. I spent a lot of time composin' the words, an while I was resting' on a minor track which led to the Diamond V, a fellow came along who was going there.'

'What sort of a fellow?' Logan scratched his greasy scalp with broken black nails.

Wagner, who was watching Red's intent face, grinned again. 'He was a travellin' barber an' dentist. A man named Dixie Malone.'

While Logan divested this information, Wagner fingered his chin, which was free from stubble. Logan pointed an accusing finger at him.

'You stayed with him long enough to have him give you a shave!'

'I did not,' Jake retorted. 'I didn't stay that long because I didn't want him to remember my face. So there. I gave myself a shave by a creek later that evenin'. An' these cuts don't have anything to do with a razor. They happened when I came through that glass window. They're slow to heal.'

The earth room went quiet. Logan looked as if he had lost interest, but the opposite, of course, was the case.

'I wrapped up the note in a small parcel, along with the ring. Malone had orders to deliver it, an' that was all.'

Logan was thinking about his next question when Wagner resumed. 'I said in the note that Dick had fallen into the hands of enemies of the family. I said not to make the matter known, but to put an insert in the county paper about payin' twenty thousand dollars for the Bonanza Minin' Company, an' then waitin' for a contact.'

Red Vargo whistled at the amount. Logan teased him about the air in the dugout being rarified, and then asked: 'Do you recall the exact words you used in the note?'

Wagner frowned, looked anxious for a moment, and finally grinned. He produced from his shirt pocket a tattered piece of paper with an exact copy of the message on it. While Logan read it, he looked away, thinking that a word or two of praise would be fully justified.

'All right, so its a good message. But you took a risk in havin' a copy of it in your pocket. Somebody might have connected you with the snatch!'

Wagner wanted to argue, but the comment had rocked his confidence and finally he didn't bother. He recovered the note and set fire to it with the tip of his cigarette.

An hour later, the trio were on the move. Logan had made up his mind quickly, and they were moving towards the north-east. Since the excitement about the ransom note, the talk had been about the imminent arrival of Doublejack Murphy in the area and the special rendezvous point which was a disused mine.

Red had his hands free, but his feet were tied underneath the palomino's barrel. Some men might have tried to give their captors the slip early in the ride, but the prisoner's confidence was not that high. He felt sure that in ordinary circumstances they would devise some form of retaliation which would put him back in their power without the use of guns. The stumble when he had first been captured was still fresh in his memory.

He had though a lot about his plight since the capture, and now he proposed to take a gamble by revealing his true identity. His feelings were that when Murphy arrived and other outlaws, it would be much more difficult to divert the gang than at present.

Logan was in the lead when Red opened up. 'I've got news for you men, news you might do well to listen to.'

Butch glanced back briefly. 'Let me guess, Pa ain't got that sort of money no more. He gambled it away at the race track, so he's poor an' his bank really owns the Diamond V.'

Red cleared his throat and began. 'The owner of the Diamond V has money, but he ain't my father. I'm a nephew, an' a poor one at that. All I have is a smallholdin' at the far end of Raich Vargo's territory. It could be that you are wastin' your time, seein' as how my Pa is dead, an' he never did nothin' to make folks admire the Vargos.'

Logan dropped back, and Wagner came closer, at the rear.

The former said: 'Gil Vargo was *your* father?'

'I don't believe you,' Wagner blustered. 'We sent the Vargo ring to identify you. You're jest tryin' to put us off, but it won't work, mister. You're the Vargo with the big nose — you answer the description all right.'

Red grinned quite broadly now. 'He knew that he was the one with the red hair. Known as Red, in the family.' He lifted his hat and glanced from one to the other of them. 'An' about that ring. Rancher Vargo will know who's been kidnapped, because the ring had my initial on the inside. A big R.'

Logan came right back and reined in alongside of Red. He studied his features from close up. 'If what you say is true, you could have deliberately put yourself in our hands. But what sort of a fool would put himself up to be kidnapped?'

'Maybe a man who owed his kin a favour.'

Red grinned quite broadly now. He knew that he had got through to the more intelligent of the two with his doubts. For his trouble Logan flicked him across the face with his reins. The ride was resumed in the same order, at a slightly faster rate of progress.

★   ★   ★

Two hours later, the new hideout was between four and five miles nearer. There had been little talk between the kidnappers and the time was surely due for a rest to refresh the horses. Red gave the appearance of a tired man. His head was drooping part way towards his chest, but his senses were keen. They were on a downward track. Some two hundred yards lower, on the north-western side, sunlight glinted on the waters of a moving stream. Timber and fern grew on the downward slope. The foliage broke up the landscape; at the same time, they prevented a desperate man from knowing whether there were concealed rocks protruding from the earth.

The sight of water had heartened

Red. He felt that his earlier revelations had given his captors plenty to think about. He was also sure that they would not be deterred from carrying out their plan. Shaken they might have been, but they were hanging on to the idea that Raich Vargo would pay out whoever they happened to have their hands on.

Red was a fine swimmer. He figured that every hour that went by the meeting with Doublejack Murphy came nearer and his own chances of making a move were receding. At the bottom of this path they would be alongside of the water and the party would assuredly stop.

He was prepared to take a big chance to get away. He felt that if he could reach that water, he might make it away. He licked his dry lips, pretending to rouse a little and looked around him. Wagner had his attention upon something in his saddle-bag. Maybe this was Red's chance. Logan was intent upon the down-trail.

Everything depended upon the palomino, the ankle thong, and luck!

He clicked his tongue very quietly, saw a response when the palomino's ears twitched, and suddenly he acted. He pulled the big horse sideways, urged it through a gap in the track-side foliage and then he was on his way. A low branch flipped off his borrowed hat and reminded him to duck. The palomino was snickering fearfully and taking large but cautious steps amid the thick fern. He drove it on, knowing full well the dangers to both of them which the desperate plunge incurred.

Wagner shouted a hoarse warning, and Logan fired a bullet high into the trees. Birds scattered, the horse swerved to avoid a tree bole and then swerved again. The deadly dodging game was on. Lesser branches tore at Red's shirt. He rode in a tensed fashion with his back arched and his eyes half closed.

More bullets followed. At least one of his captors had ridden into the foliage in pursuit.

Inevitably, the time came when the horse missed its footing. It rolled, just as another deterring bullet came rather close. Above all, Red did not want to be caught with a leg trapped in thick, treacherous foliage. He tensed himself for what was to follow.

He was aware of every little movement of the fall. The thong snapped just at the critical moment when his leg was being pinned and his body had to go with it. For a few seconds the horse writhed. He wondered if it had injured a limb. Suddenly it rose again, and blundered off further down the slope, apparently unhurt.

At this, Red seized his chance. He darted away from the horse's path, racing along in a crouching position and getting steadily nearer to the tantalising water just below him. Some thirty yards separated horse and man when the animal pulled up alongside of the stream, and Red slithered to a halt on knees and elbows.

The pursuit was still at his back. He

saw that he would have to keep moving if he was to stay free. Before the pursuit could identify his exact position, he stood up, took a deep breath, and dived neatly into the tempting waters. His trajectory took him down deep.

10

Butch Logan did not dismount until he was alongside of the water. And when he touched the ground, he was breathless. In coming down that treacherous slope on horseback he had taken an awful chance. Any man in that sort of territory with a lame horse was in an unenviable position, but an outlaw might as well give himself up if anyone was looking for him.

Logan counted himself lucky to have reached the bank without injury. Screened by a large willow, he glanced up and down stream and wondered what Vargo had done with himself. In the past half hour or so, he had built up a great feeling of anger towards Red. Firstly, he had deliberately set himself up as their victim. He had hoodwinked them into thinking that he was the all-important Vargo heir, and now he had deliberately made a break for freedom, having declared who he was. Doubtless, he still thought that he was immune from a fast bullet because of his name and the tie-up with the kidnap.

The swarthy outlaw believed Red's revelations. Moreover, he had thought about Raich Vargo and the feelings of the honest Vargos when renegade Gil brought their family name into disrepute. Logan really thought that the rancher might not pay out to save his shamed brother's son. In this reasoning, he was wrong, but he was not to know it.

To the rear, he could hear Jake coming down rather noisily on foot. Wagner had abandoned his mount at trail level. Now he was wondering how Logan would react to the breakaway attempt. As Wagner had been bringing up the rear, he ought to have been the first to react when Red made a break for it. Actually, he had called out first, but would Butch think that he had done all that could have been expected of him?

As Red continued to stay out of sight, Butch forced himself to concentrate on where he might be. Clearly, the bank opposite was steep and muddy, and Vargo would have been lucky to scramble out on that side before Butch arrived. Therefore, he might have gone with the current, in this case towards the left; or, he might be hiding somewhere, his body shielded by water or foliage. Butch favoured the latter theory.

Shortly before Wagner reached him, he turned his bay gelding so that it faced upstream and sent it off in that direction with a few timely slaps on the rump. As the bay moved off, Wagner, drawn by the sound, called softly. Logan ignored him. Instead of answering, Butch moved a little closer to the water's edge. He went down on one knee, his rifle to hand, and gradually sprawled out under the concealing branches of a willow.

All the time from then on, Logan was watching the stream's surface and the opposite bank. The ripples on the surface made it difficult to see far into the water, but he stuck to his task.

Wagner blundered out further upstream, drawn in his search by the departing bay. He was breathing hard, and obviously not enjoying himself at all because he was out of touch. After a short lapse of time, he started to come back. Presently, he almost stumbled over one of Logan's boots and that brought a sharp retort from the prone man.

'Doggone it, Jake! Can't you be careful? Take a walk downstream an' act as though I'm not here. You hear me?'

Wagner paused a few feet away. He could tell by Logan's attitude that he was now prepared to shoot to kill. Their joint kidnapping enterprise was at an end, one way or another. Jake hesitated, wondering whether it was worthwhile to argue with Butch about shooting their former prisoner.

Suddenly Logan turned around, and saw that in addition to carrying weapons Wagner was toting along the stetson which had been brushed from Vargo's head at the top of the slope. Anger consumed the dark-haired man.

He said through his teeth, 'Drop that hat, an' get on with your business like I told you. Or else!'

The threat was clearly visible. Wagner dropped the hat and moved off downstream without another word. He made a little noise on the way, so as to draw attention away from Butch's hiding place. Jake's morale had suffered again. He did not think that they would see Red again, and he did not think trying an ambush alongside of this water would do either his partner or himself any good.

If Logan did not behave foolishly, it would be possible to join up with Murphy again without his knowing that they had made a mess of a private kidnap attempt. Wagner sighed. He walked on, slowly and carefully, until he came to a depression in the bank, there he sat down to await developments.

Red who had anticipated serious trouble after his escape attempt, had acted wisely since he entered the water. Instead of trying to make any sort of distance downstream, where his enemies would doubtless look for him, he had swum across to the other bank and hidden himself as best he could under the down-drooping, slender, pliant branches of the willows.

By gripping two or three branches, the tips of which were actually in the water, he was able to hold himself in check as the current tugged at him. Scrambling out would be exceedingly difficult without the use of the trees. It would not do to make his move in a hurry, otherwise he might give himself away.

He kept telling himself that lots of patience would be needed to throw off these two determined outlaws, and he felt that he had ample self-discipline to see him through. He leaned back until only his eyes, mouth and nostrils were above water. He could not turn his head without throwing up one or two small ripples, and he did not have the use of his ears. But he was safe for the moment, and that helped.

★ ★ ★

Twenty minutes went by. In that time, Red had grown tired of his prolonged posture under the willow tree. He had no means of knowing how far the searchers had gone, but he believed that they had moved further afield, and that they were confining their seach to the trail-side of the stream.

With his growing impatience came confidence. Logan and Wagner would not stay around forever. The palomino was somewhere downstream, beyond his reach, but perhaps the time had now come when he might haul himself out on to the bank and dry himself out a little.

He thought about it for two or three

minutes, and then decided. About eighteen inches above his head there was a branch which would take his weight, or part of it. He would use that one to haul himself partially clear and then swing in towards the bole of the tree. After that, a slow climb upwards and a further climb out over the bank. And then rest and a slow dry-out, and other plans, such as the recovery of the horse . . .

★ ★ ★

Logan's pockmarked countenance was a sea of perspiration. He had looked for a long time and seen nothing. Soon, Wagner would be back and Jake would rub it in if the silent ambush failed. The onetime butcher began to grind his teeth. He pulled off his hat and savaged his quiff, and just as he replaced the hat he saw, or thought he saw, a movement on the opposite bank.

He blinked salt sweat out of his eyes and looked again, concentrating on the

153

same spot. After a brief pause his rubbery lips spread in an unholy grin. What he had seen was a man's arm coming up out of the water and gripping a part of the tree. A slight sway in the branches had given away the swimmer.

At once, Logan began to edge the Henry into a better position for shooting. While he was busy, another arm came out of the water, followed by Red's dripping head and neck. Logan talked to his weapon, his lips moving without sound. He waited for the upper part of the chest to clear the water and then he was ready.

He sighted carefully and squeezed. The weapon bucked against his shoulder. After the brief muzzle flame the first bullet winged its way across the stream's surface. A hand slipped from the bough. At once Logan levered and fired again. His second shot was also on target. His third hit only a hand, the last part of the victim's body to slide back into the water. Red, who was almost dead, turned over in the water and began to float downstream. The current drew him away from the bank and urged him further into the stream.

★　★　★

At the time of the first flurry of shots, Dick Vargo was between one and two miles away from the scene of the break.

Dick had spent a lot of monotonous time searching out the hiding place where he felt Red was being held. After failing to find it, he refused to give up and instead moved further away from the area. It was a stretch of the same stream where the killing had taken place that drew Dick along.

He, himself, was a poor performer in water, but Red, on the other hand, was an accomplished swimmer. If Red saw the chance of making a break he would make every possible use of the water. It was a part of his way of thinking. Thus mildly comforted in his perplexity, Dick had stayed close to the stream and followed it along for a few miles.

He was dozing against a rock when the staccato rattle of gun fire aroused him around two-fifteen in the afternoon. The gun shots put him on his mettle. He saw to his weapons and found a better hiding place on the side of the stream.

All he could associate the shooting with was a possible break for freedom. If Red had made that break, then he was close to the river and he had some sort of plan, however feeble, with which to get further away from his enemies. The chances were very much against his going upstream, and that consideration kept Dick where he was.

Dick was every bit as watchful as Logan could be, although he had a wider area to survey. Perhaps a half hour had gone by when the second outburst of rifle fire came echoing downstream. The listener could not be at all clear, but he thought that the last bout of shooting was nearer stream level.

Again, he wondered if he should not try and make his way further upstream. Not much liking himself, he decided against it. In broad daylight, he could very well blunder straight into trouble and that would not do Red any good at all.

Time dragged after that. At times, Dick wished that someone would shoot again, so that his flagging spirits would not become altogether depressed. He was disappointed. The sounds of nature closed in around him and stayed that way.

The sight of the hat floating downstream made him rub his eyes and look again. He blinked several times and what his eyes told him was rather frightening. It looked like his own hat, the one Red had taken from him in the hotel. The coined band was visible, although it was almost soaked.

Of course, it did not mean finally that the head which had last worn it now had no further use for it. But Dick had to admit to himself that he was dismayed by it. He could not stop himself from thinking that it had been tossed into the water, rather than that it had floated off a swimmer's head.

In order to recover it, he had to throw a loop out into the stream. Fortunately, he touched it and started to draw it inshore the first time. He searched it for messages, found none, and settled back to wait for some other indication of his cousin's fate.

★ ★ ★

The floating body started to approach some time after four o'clock. Dick's mouth dried out. Almost at once he started to feel mildly sick. Grim resolution made him toss aside his Winchester, and wade into the water.

Red was floating face downwards. There was never the slightest doubt that he was dead. The last lot of gunfire must have killed him. It was not hard to guess how he had died; on the point of leaving the water.

Dick grabbed him by the leather vest, a part of his own wardrobe, and slowly hauled him inshore. The bank, fortunately, was easy to negotiate at that point. Red had scratches on his face, a bloody hand, and two bullets in the upper part of his chest. His facial expression was not a happy one.

For a time, Dick's mind would not function. He built a small fire to give him a little comfort, and did all in his powers to distract himself from any consideration of the killers upstream. Red would have to be buried, and Dick had no stomach for trying to get him across to Diamond V territory in that stricken state.

He began to make plans to bury his cousin in the nearest bit of yielding ground. One hour after the discovery of the corpse he began his task. The work of digging acted as a sort of therapy. He worked at it, and watched the level gradually deepen.

As he struggled with the earth, his thoughts cleared. He tried to assemble

159

facts to cover the shooting of Red. Maybe they had learned, after all, that Red was the son of Gil Vargo, and that he was of no particular kidnap value. His thoughts ranged on, considering this and that, and trying to keep away from the fact that Red had repaid a favour with his life.

The floor of the grave was just about the right level when Dick got the first intimation that he was not alone by the stream. Too late, he thought about tossing down the spade and reaching for weapons. Unfortunately, he had discarded his shirt, side-arms and everything that impeded his digging.

Wagner loomed up in front of him, on horseback, a rifle at the ready. Being led behind the lean gunman was the palomino, from which Dick had been parted too long. Some five seconds later, a rifle clicked in another direction, and Logan revealed himself, even closer.

Dick spat to one side of the grave, ignoring the menace of the guns. He walked past Wagner and did not stop walking until he was alongside of the pale horse, which greeted him affectionately. Wagner was a little nonplussed by this seeming indifference to the gun threat, but Logan, oddly enough, was chuckling to himself.

'Jake, I guess we're back in business. Meet the true owner of that there pale hoss. Dick Vargo, in the flesh. An' takin' time out to bury his cousin, who treated us badly back there on the trail. Howdy, Vargo? We sure are glad to meet you.'

Dick shot Logan a glance of pure venom. He then ignored the outlaws while he finished the grave, and lowered Red into it. Even Logan was surprised at the ex-cavalryman's absorption with his task. A whole hour went by, during which the renegades boiled coffee on the fire and made themselves a passable meal.

Dick filled in all the soil he had dug out. Next he made a small cross out of pieces of driftwood and stuck it in the mound at the head of the grave. The usual details were carved on it, and then, drooping a little with weariness, Dick approached the fire and partook of coffee and food.

When his meal was finished, he asked the names of the two outlaws. After a brief pause, Logan supplied the information.

Half an hour later, they started to pack up for a little more trail following. Dick returned to the grave and was busy there for a few minutes. When they were mounted up and ready to leave, Jake Wagner walked his stallion closer to the mound and took a look at the words carved on the wood.

Dick had added a few more since the meal. The addition said: *Murdered this day by two outlaws, Butch Logan and Jake Wagner*.

11

Working independently, and with little knowledge to guide him, Slim Petersen was nevertheless conducting his own individual search for the Vargo boys more or less in the right area. His spirited dash across the more direct Medicine Creek-Cottonwood trail had put him into terrain which was further north than Logan and Wagner had operated in this far.

Slim was conscious of the passing of the days, and the need for a notice to be put in the local newspaper, the *Thompson Telegraph*, located in the county seat, Thompson Falls. It was a good thing that the *Telegraph* only came out once a week, and that he had a few days in hand before he was forced to relay Raich Vargo's message. If time became an even greater factor, Slim felt sure that he could get the message through to the newspaper by telegraph, and thus save himself a headlong dash to county seat when he particularly wanted to be elsewhere.

During the day which was so fateful for the Vargo cousins, Slim roamed backwards and forwards over a huge triangle of almost untenable ground, using all the high spots to look further in the hope of detecting the delicate touch of man.

His efforts were so unrewarding as to make him feel lonely. On two occasions during that day, he had the distinct feeling that he was being observed himself, and yet he had not the slightest inkling as to what had caused the feeling.

Was it something to do with the trail-rider's sixth sense, or was he merely thinking likely and unlikely things due to his rooted feelings of loneliness? Nothing happened in daylight to deepen this feeling and, as the hours of early evening mellowed the day, Slim sought out for himself a camping sight in the bottom of a dried-out *arroyo*. He had to dig for water, in the centre of the gorge, but he thought the effort was worth it when the water appeared and it did not taste too brackish.

Soon, he had a fire and a meal on the way, and for an hour or two he proposed to put the Vargo problems out of his mind. He ate his bacon and biscuits and drank quite a liberal amount of coffee; it was when he dipped into his hatband for a match to light his smoke that he came upon Raich Vargo's letter. At that moment, his thoughts returned to Vargo business, and, in particular, to his search.

The sky was still bright in the west when he reread the message and brooded over the trust which the ageing rancher had placed in him. The very words of the message filled Slim with pride. He felt that at last he had made contact with a rancher for whom he could feel an unreserved respect.

The letter said: *This is to tell who it*

may concern that the Bearer, Slim Petersen, is hereby given my full authority. If he asks for funds, he is to be given up to $20,000.

Witness my ring, and if necessary, telegraph

Lyndon Groves, banker, of Medicine Creek.

                    (signed) *Raich Vargo.*
                    Diamond V Ranch,
                    Clovis County,
                    New Mexico Territory.

Slim said to the sky: 'The bearer, Slim Petersen, is hereby given my full authority. If he asks for funds, to be given up to twenty thousand dollars.'

It occurred to Slim as he read this that no man in his lifetime had shown so much confidence in him. This little piece of paper, along with the ring, was really dynamite. It meant that he, Slim, could walk into a bank, and ask for twenty thousand dollars on the say-so of Raich Vargo, a man he had not known for much more than an hour.

He held up the note, above his head,

where a light breeze blew on it. At that moment, as it moved in the grip of his finger and thumb he realised that if it and the ring fell into the wrong hands another man might take advantage of the written message and come out twenty thousand dollars the richer.

This thought made him whistle. What, for instance, could Walter Legrange do with twenty thousand dollars? He realised as soon as he had thought about it, that this was improper speculation. The sort which had to be nipped before it grew in a man's head and turned his thoughts from the strictly honest to the dishonest.

He sat up, and was about to replace the note in his pocket when he thought better of it. Instead, he wrapped it in a piece of old newspaper which usually filled out his hatband, and placed it under a stone a short distance from the fire.

Shortly after that, he took a walk around his small domain, and for the third time that day he got the impression that he might not be entirely alone. The dun was passive enough, but did that necessarily negative Slim's distinct impression?

As he knelt beside the fire, he reminded himself of the importance of his self-imposed task, and of an old saying which he learned from the lips of Pop Legrange. Something which meant that it was better to be a live coward tomorrow than a dead hero today. Rather belatedly, he decided to act upon Legrange's proverb.

He knelt beside his roll, doffed his hat and started to build an effigy of himself with the saddle as a base. Shortly after that, he collected his weapons, his water bottle and a spy glass and went off up the *arroyo*, far beyond the camping area.

Some four hundred yards up the winding depression, he rose cautiously to his feet and began to push his way in a prone position through the yellowed grass. A short distance using that form of travel quickly tired him out.

He thought better of working his way

into a position which afforded a distant view of the fire, and sank down, determined to sleep come what may.

Around midnight, he thought he heard the dun snicker, but there was no follow up to the sound, so he sank down again and resumed his sleep. Perhaps a half hour later, a heavy shoulder weapon started to pump shells into the camp beside the fire.

The side-rolled hat leapt under the impact. A blanket was holed in three places and the saddle acquired a couple of unwanted grooves. Slim awoke quickly. He got as far as his knees before his startled senses told him that his would-be assassin was on the other side of the *arroyo*.

In seeking to be smart, he had crawled out of the depression on the wrong side. That being so, it would be difficult to get to grips with the lethal gunman who had attacked him with no apparent reason. After giving the matter a lot of thought, Slim came to the conclusion that he had been attacked because his presence in the area presented a threat to a person or persons unknown.

He yawned, thought about what he ought to do, and finally came round to the idea of trying to stalk the man who had fired the gun. After all, it was a reasonable assumption that the gunman might have contact with the kidnappers. He might be a kidnapper himself. In which case, an effort to make contact with him might lead to something worthwhile.

With this in mind, Slim made a large circuit of the grassed terrain on his side of the *arroyo*, his aim being to cross it perhaps a couple of furlongs on the other side of the fire, and thus come upon the marksman, always supposing that he stayed somewhere near for the rest of the night.

★　★　★

Slim's attacker, however, was a very tricky customer to deal with on a dark night. He was a stocky, thick-set man in his late thirties with the sort of gait which made night movement seem natural for humans.

Lucky Parradine had been all kinds of man in the past. His two main occupations had helped form his character. He was a one-time animal trapper. His skills in matching his cunning against animals sometimes tired, and, when he had no men to hunt, he looked for men in towns to gamble with.

Certain fortuitous meetings had given him successful outlaws as his friends. They had learned about his special skills at a time when they particularly needed protection from careful pursuers. He had won their affection and regard through his talent for rubbing out trails and constructing false ones. Everyone knew that his night vision was second to none.

Shortly after the shoot-up of Slim's bed roll Parradine quietly broke cover and trotted forward quite silently in a pair of plains Indians' mocassins. Although he was moving fairly fast, he never once put his foot upon a twig, the cracking of which might have given away his presence.

His body was encompassed in a fur cap and a thick plaid coat, but neither of these overheated or otherwise hampered his body as he moved to the edge of the fire and regarded the scene of his handiwork. In a matter of seconds, he saw that he had shot up a roll without a body in it, but that did not prevent him from looking around the camping spot before retiring.

His movements were quick, agile ones. Sometimes he was fully stretched, and others he was crouched down. A man seeking to kill him from a distance would have found him a difficult target. As the seconds passed, and no retaliation, Parradine began to feel more at ease, but he did not relax.

Not until he had searched the area as another thief might have gone over a hotel bedroom did he straighten up and think about moving off again. The man who had made this camp had gone up in his estimation. He had pulled out, entirely unseen, and to give Parradine the slip in that fashion called for a high degree of skill.

Lucky paused with the paper he had found just beyond the flickering extent of the firelight. He had only fired upon the stranger because he had persisted in searching this area so close to the old mine workings which the Murphy outfit were planning to use as an important rendezvous. That the fellow had got away did not much matter to Parradine; unless he had been marked down for disposal by some of the other outlaws advancing into the area.

Apart from the paper, the intruder left things as they were. He moved out of the stream bed and trotted back in the direction from which he had come, seeing no one and himself unseen. Near to the spot where he had left his mount, he went to a badger hole, long since abandoned. With his head well below the level of the land, he lit a match and perused the paper.

As he read and digested the words of Raich Vargo, he began to see that he might have stumbled upon something of real value. Apparently, the man he had attacked had some sort of title to twenty thousand dollars.

Parradine, who needed far less sleep than the average man, at once considered his find. He made up his mind quickly, and set off in the direction of the mine workings, acting upon the supposition that some of his own renegade friends might have need of the knowledge he possessed.

He took his bearings very carefully and broke camp, running for the first mile ahead of his mount. About a mile clear of the mine workings, he became aware of the presence of other humans. This new knowledge made him change course for the new objective. He approached cautiously, and was gratified to find that he knew the identity of the drowsy man leaning on a rifle beside a swale bottom fire.

Some twenty yards away, Parradine stopped walking carefully and deliberately rattled a couple of stones under his feet. Wagner came to his feet rather slowly and put his gun to his shoulder. The newcomer stopped his forward progress before the challenge, and called out to the challenger.

'Well, hello, old friend Jake, you wouldn't fire on Lucky Parradine, would you? An old friend who is so keen to see you again. Besides, I may have brought you some interestin' news. Do you know anybody by the name of Vargo?'

Wagner and Parradine were still shaking hands when the name was mentioned. It was sufficient to arouse the sleeping figure on the other side of the fire. Wagner gripped Parradine's arm, and glanced warningly at his prisoner. He asked what Lucky's interest was in the Vargo family and was shown the scrap of paper.

Parradine paraphrased it for Wagner,

who then took it nearer the fire to read it for himself. He read it aloud, which gave Dick the gist of what was going on.

'You mean you located this, this Slim Petersen, today? Is he . . . ?'

'No, he aint dead, Jake. But he might have been. You see, he was roamin' about in this area, too close to the mine for comfort. So I aimed a few shots at him after dark. Only he wasn't in his roll. A real smart hombre, Petersen must be. Do you mind tellin' me why you're so interested in this Vargo's note?'

Wagner glanced down at Dick. He moved further away, taking Parradine with him. 'Because Butch an' me, we snatched this Vargo, an' we're holdin' him to ransom. The man you fired on was the older Vargo's representative. It's a good job you didn't kill him. It might have prevented us from gettin' the pay-off money.'

Parradine was excited now. He turned towards the fire and whipped off his fur cap. With a wide-toothed comb he started to smooth out his short dark hair. His close-trimmed beard and moustache received the same treatment and all the time his black button-like eyes were darting sudden glances at the fire, and the prisoner and elsewhere.

'But if we have the note givin' the authority, Jake, ain't we in a strong position? Can't we dispense with the Petersen fellow, and do the chasin' ourselves?'

Jake shook his head very decidedly. 'I don't think that would do at all, Lucky, you see we don't have the ring, and without that we might be in a fix.'

Parradine thought hard for another two or three minutes. 'So you want this man, Petersen, to go ahead with the assignment the rancher gave him? Is that right?'

'That's about the size of the matter,' Jake replied calmly. With Butch away from the camp he was acting much more rationally.

'In that case, I'll jest have to go back

to the camp an' put the letter back where I found it. Leave it to me. Petersen wasn't near the camp when I came away. It'll be all right.'

Parradine rested for five minutes, during which time he warmed his hands at the fire, and ate lightly and drank coffee. He was then ready for the return journey. One moment he was there, and another he had melted into the darkness beyond the firelight.

12

An hour before dawn, Slim Petersen was a very tired young man. He had made his wide detour around the *arroyo*, and for his pains he was no wiser. Once or twice he thought he had detected a slight movement on the opposite side of the gorge, but nothing had happened to confirm his first impressions.

He had dozed from time to time, through sheer fatigue and having to move in an unaccustomed way. The night coolness had also bothered him, so that he never actually crossed over on to the other side of the *arroyo*.

While the day was dawning further east, Slim's head was propped on his forearm. His bandanna was fluttering in a light breeze and his hair was also ruffled. When the dawn chorus of birds began to rouse him his eyelids were heavy and his best concentration was far gone.

He thought that perhaps his attacker might move in again upon the camp around dawn, but nothing of the kind happened. Slim crossed the gorge and started to move up it on the side from which the attack had come. Birds, and small animal sounds on that side more or less confirmed that his attacker had left, and eventually he straightened and walked cautiously back to his starting point.

The fire was reduced to embers. Dust had blown around and his gear looked thoroughly disturbed, but he knew that the disturbance had been mostly caused by the bullets. He picked up his stetson, a good three dollar hat, and found that a bullet had passed through the curled up brim on both sides.

One after another he explored the three holes in the blanket and finally fingered the unwanted grooves in his saddle. He sat down and sighed discontentedly. His stomach was rumbling with emptiness, but the most disconcerting thing of all was not getting within sighting distance of the fellow who had sought to kill him.

He stood up again and rekindled the fire. He was thinking that since he had crossed trails with the Vargos life certainly had been hectic. It was as though the Vargos were his kin, rather than Walter Legrange and Maria. He thought fleetingly of the homesteader and the girl he had grown up with, and then the Vargo problems claimed his mind again.

Two attempts on his life in a mere few days. First a knife attack and now a night ambush with weapons. And no progress to speak of. No clear idea as to where the kidnapped man was. Nothing to tell Raich Vargo, if he popped up in a hurry and asked for a progress report.

A sudden thought occurred to Slim. The note! When he went off up the *arroyo* the night before he had left it under a stone. It might have blown away, or have been shifted by a stray bullet. He rushed to the spot where he had hidden it in the small piece of newspaper. It was not there! Frantically, he started to search around for it. To his surprise he found it about a yard away, under another stone and with some of the newspaper wrapping missing.

That was a puzzle for a tired man on an empty stomach. But the short letter was intact. He walked about rubbing the tip of his chin with it while he thought about the immediate future. The time factor bothered him. The way things were beginning to shape up it began to look as though Raich Vargo would have to forfeit the money.

There were only two or three days before the next issue of the *Thompson Telegraph* came out, and before that weekly issue appeared Slim had to make contact with the editor and have Mr. Vargo's message about the Bonanza Mining Company printed. If the acknowledgement did not go in the press, then all kinds of other complications might occur in the matter of the kidnap.

Slim narrowed his eyes and thought about the settlements in the district.

There was Cottonwood, of course, to the north. He could get in touch with Thompson Falls from there by telegraph, but perhaps it would be better, more thorough if he made the trip into Thompson Falls on horseback and kept a lookout for developments there.

It was a longish ride which would take him the best part of two days. He would be riding away from the area of the kidnap, and that did not seem right. Eventually, however, he decided that he would best be serving Raich Vargo if he went along with the message himself.

There was another consideration. He might have to draw the money on the rancher's behalf, and Thompson was the place where the withdrawal would have to be made, as Medicine was a little too far way.

Slim groaned and muttered to himself, the sort of behaviour which was usually foreign to him. But he had come to a decision. He prepared a hurried breakfast and resolutely thought about the long haul to Thompson.

At three in the afternoon on the following day, Slim walked his tired dun into the western outskirts of the county seat. It was clear to anyone who cared to look that he had done many miles that day. He cared nothing for his appearance at the outset. His half-closed eyes were studying the false fronts in the hope of seeing a board which suggested the newspaper. He did not see what he wanted at first. A water trough in the shade drew the horse. He dismounted, hitched it to the rail in reaching distance of the trough, and rocked his saddle.

At the first intersection, he called for one beer, drank it and asked where the newspaper was to be found. A condescending barman informed him that the next issue would not be on the street until the following evening, and Slim thanked him in a rather curt fashion.

The *Thompson Telegraph* offices and workshop were on Second Street, the thoroughfare further north than

Main. He knocked some of the dust out of his hat and wandered up the two steps which gave access to the building.

A small round-faced man with spectacles and greased down dark hair was leaning against a bench just inside and smoking a pipe. He looked to be about fifty. The press was still and the interior was quiet, but there was no mistaking it for anything else because of the smell of printer's ink.

'What can I do for you, stranger?'

Slim nodded, removed his hat and rested his weight on the edge of a desk cluttered with papers. 'I'd like to put a short message in your personal column for the next issue. Could that be arranged?'

The newspaper owner grinned with the pipe in his mouth. He nodded and moved round to the seat behind the desk. 'What was the nature of your message, mister?'

'I'll dictate it to you, if you like. Are you ready? 'Mr. Raich Vargo, rancher in this county, agrees to pay $20,000 for the Bonanza Mine Holdings Company. Instructions awaited.' Got all that?'

The writer extracted his pipe, and cleared his throat. He read out the message which he had taken down. Slim nodded when he was satisfied, and asked what the charge would be. Money changed hands and the young man left the office.

His feet were moving more slowly than usual as he found a stall in a livery for his horse and a room in a hotel for himself. He cleaned himself in a leisurely fashion and with a clean shirt on his back he finally went in search of food.

Fifteen minutes after he had entered the restaurant, a familiar face squinted in through the steamy window. The man hesitated, half made up his mind to give the place a miss, and then came in. Slim, who was sitting well back at a small table with a plate of hot food in front of him, rose to his feet, full of interest.

Something made him not use the name of the newcomer. 'Over here, sir,' he called in a friendly voice.

Raich Vargo turned in his direction and almost at once the scowl left his face. He had come to town specially to see Slim, and now he had found him. A waiter arrived while they were getting the usual pleasantries out of the way. Vargo ordered a steak without looking up, and they were left alone.

Although he was hungry, Slim was as interested in what he had to tell his employer as he was in the food. Slim's plate was empty and the rancher was half way through his steak by the time the narrative came to an end.

'By the way, Mr. Vargo, what made you come to the county seat, after all?'

'Slim, I guess you could answer that for yourself. All my life I've been an active man, and now, with my family under pressure I jest couldn't stay away.' He patted the broad belt at his waist. 'An' what's more I've brought along the ransom money, so you won't need to go hawkin' that note round, after all.'

After a brief silence, Slim remarked: 'I would say that kidnappers are greedy men as well as bein' ruthless.' Encouraged by his listener to go on, he resumed. 'I don't think they'll wait another week to give us instructions in the paper. I'd say they'll put something in the mail office. What if they try to contact you at home?'

'In that case, someone will get in touch with me right away. Maybe we could have another talk with that newspaper man, later on, an' if he don't get a high priority message in this issue, then we'll watch the mail office.'

'You think it's possible they could get a message in *this* issue?'

'Why not? All they have to do is go along there an' ask the editor if there's anything in this week's issue from Raich Vargo. If he let's them see what it is, then they could put their instructions in right away. I agree with you, they're greedy, an' they won't wait long.'

Early next morning, the rancher and Slim had their talk with the newspaper man. His issue was not on the street, but he confirmed that there was no reply as yet for the Bonanza business, and that he would be unable to print any last minute message.

A short while later, Vargo contacted a couple of prominent townsmen well known to himself. One of them was the man in charge of the mail office, which occupied the upper floor of a building down the east end of Main. As a result of the discussions, Slim found himself installed that same evening in the rearmost of the two mail offices as a temporary guard.

The scheme which Vargo had put in hand was one in which to keep a close check on the comings and goings of people who used the mail office. Vargo, himself, was going to watch during the day, and Slim was on duty during the closed hours.

In addition to this, one or the other was to make a daily check at the newspaper office to make sure that no message had been left there.

At eleven in the evening, Slim strolled out of Second Street and into Main. He moved up from the intersection at a smart pace and let himself into the mail office building by a side entrance. It was dark and shadowy, and once the door was closed again, the distant sounds of merriment in the saloons was muffled. Slim felt very much alone.

He sniffed the dust of the unfamiliar block and started cautiously up the inside staircase. A door led out into the rear office which had no special function except possibly as a sorting room at times when the mail delivery was heavy. He almost fell over the chair which was to take his weight during his night vigil, and caught it just in time, preventing a big clatter.

Having recovered his poise and improved his night vision he wandered through into the main office and took a long look at the big counter which was in the shape of a long arc, almost a

190

quarter of a circle. At the back of it were the many cubby holes with letters of the alphabet underneath them. Here and there were a few uncollected letters, but there was nothing in the part marked with a 'V'.

There were windows along the front. For a minute or two, Slim stood behind them watching the glow of the lamp-lit windows and the casual comings and goings of late night roisterers. He soon tired of this sort of observation and withdrew himself to the rear.

He denied himself a cigarette and at once started to fit his body into the chair. It had a high back and open wooded arms. As he tilted it back against the wall and pushed his hat forward his thoughts were on the comfortable hotel bed which awaited him in another part of the town.

He rubbed the back of his head against the wall. One pleasing conclusion came out of this. His head was better. He had been in and around the Vargos long enough for the original injury to heal. He hoped that he would not get another one in its place, and slowly his breathing deepened. His body craved for sleep, and he would achieve it, even though he was in a difficult position.

The slight breeze coming under the communicating door eventually roused him after an hour or so. He slowly blinked himself awake. He pondered over the breeze, wondering if it had freshly sprung up, and if it had not — why had it not disturbed him earlier?

He made an effort to come fully awake and partially succeeded. The chair creaked under him as he shifted his position. His bodily aches dictated that he should take a walk. He went in the direction of the breeze, not at all convinced that anything was wrong. The door to the front office opened towards him. He stepped back, and was just going through it when a bunched fist with a strip of leather wrapped around it hit him full in the jaw.

Slim was arrested in his tracks. His

knees buckled and he went down, fighting to keep his senses. Meanwhile the owner of the fist, who had been waiting for him behind the door, slipped out by the front entrance and clattered down the outside staircase.

By the time Slim was on his feet again and fit enough to take a look around, the intruder was a blur of shadow, just slipping into the alley on the other side of the street. The aching head of the temporary guard prevented his taking up the chase sufficiently quickly to be worthwhile.

Instead, he drooped over the wide curve of the counter and gave his head a proper chance to clear. When he finally straightened up, he realised that something was different. There was now a letter in the cubby hole marked 'V'.

13

Rancher Vargo found it very difficult to sleep in the hotel bed, although the management had given him one of the best rooms and certainly the most comfortable furniture. This was the first time that he had been away from home in quite a few years. Another reason for his restlessness was the obvious one, the plight of his nephew and possibly his son.

He had read everything in the current issue of the *Telegraph* and the account of the raids in the next county further west had taken a second reading. The editor's report suggested that the vicious raids by a small band of outlaws on isolated homesteads and ranches was reminiscent of the situation a few years years earlier when the Wild Bunch ramrodded by Doublejack Murphy was on the rampage.

People were shot up and left wounded, if they resisted. The raiders took what they liked, and used what they liked and left when they were good and ready. Good riding horses were appropriated from time to time, and the outbreak of violence looked as if it had come to stay.

There was a polite query as to how long it would be before the county sheriff of Clovis County had to buckle on his weapons and run out a posse in order to try and bring the renegades to heel. Further down the page again, under a different heading, was a short paragraph which raised the query as to whether Doublejack Murphy had just been released, or not. One or two rather doubtful sources gave it as their opinion that the top outlaw had been due for release the month prior to this.

This reading about insurrections gave the rancher a cold chill down his back. He had lived a sufficient number of summers not to want to see the Wild Bunch back in action in Clovis County.

The populace, he felt sure, could do a whole lot better without the influx of those who lived by the gun.

His thoughts slipped away again to the kidnap. He started rather suddenly as a quiet knock came on the door. The newspaper rustled as he folded it and dropped it to the floor. He reached for his gun belt at the head of the bed before answering the knock.

'Who is it?'

'Slim Petersen, Mr. Vargo. There's been a development, so I locked up the building and came away. Could I possibly come in and talk to you?'

'Jest hold on a minute, Slim, I'll be right there.'

A minute later, Slim was admitted. In rather a breathless state he explained about the clash with the man in the mail office. He did nothing to cover up his own lack of perception when he walked into the sucker punch in passing through the door.

Vargo looked grave, but he was quick to prevent Slim from blaming himself excessively. 'You weren't to know that anyone had sneaked into the front part of the building. The fact is, he surprised you, but you also surprised him. In any case, I think you have more to tell. What is it?'

Slim relaxed a little, and grinned. He produced from his shirt pocket a long crumpled envelope addressed to Raich Vargo, rancher, c/o The Mail Office, Thompson Falls. He handed it over with every sign of eagerness. 'I brought this along with me. The intruder must have broken in there specially to leave it unseen. Do you think it was all right to take it off the shelves without waiting for the proper men to distribute it?'

Vargo gave a wry smile. 'If we don't cut a few corners, Slim, we're likely to lose money an' maybe one or more lives. So don't be so sensitive about it, huh?'

He held the paper some distance from his eyes, having discarded the envelope. Slim rested on the foot of the bed, controlling his curiosity with a great effort. The rancher sniffed and then read it out for him.

'To Raich Vargo, Esquire. Mr. Vargo is advised to put the $20,000 in a small parcel. He, or his representative, must ride after the Thursday stage-coach to Cottonwood and hand over the parcel to the crew at Halfway Creek for delivery to Cottonwood mail office.

'Contact must then move right away, or prisoner will not be released. Remember to obey orders.'

Having read the message, Raich looked up to see Slim's reactions. The young cowpuncher got up off the bed and began to pace up and down. The brightness of his eyes showed that he was weighing up the instructions from every angle. Presently, he stopped and faced his employer with his hands on his hips.

'Will you go through with it, jest as he says?'

'I don't have a lot of choice, do I?'

'There's a choice as to who delivers the money to the coach, and at least we know what is supposed to happen in very good time. It's Wednesday tomorrow, so we could make plans.'

Vargo sat with his stockinged feet nervously thumping the ground. He could not think of anything at all to do, other than to take along the money himself so as to minimise the risk of anything going wrong with the other part of the business, the release.

'I guess I'll have to take the parcel, Slim, an' that doesn't leave you with very much to do, does it?'

Slim stopped by the window and stared down into the street where a mongrel dog was scratching itself to dislodge a flea. He talked animatedly.

'The man who delivers that parcel to the coach knows too much from the kidnappers' point of view. He will be in danger all the time. You, if I might say so, are too valuable a man to do the delivering. You see, they might attack the messenger even before Halfway, an' then they'd kill him. If they waited till Halfway, the chances are that he would run into an ambush as soon as he was clear of the coach an' any through traffic.

'They would have to get him out of the way because he knew where the parcel was going to. Do you see what I mean?'

'I can see that you are tryin' real hard to talk yourself into the job, Slim, but if I have second thoughts an' let you go in my place, what do *I* do? How can I sit back in circumstances like these?'

'You don't have to sit back, Mr. Vargo. You could be away from here at daybreak. Ride for Cottonwood and alert the authorities there to apprehend anyone who comes looking for your parcel. You see how it might work out? The peace officers could maybe beat the truth out of them, and I, if I was lucky enough to break out of my ambush, I might get a line on the base of these pushin' raiders an' their kidnappin' friends. So what do you say?'

Vargo produced a couple of cigars

and handed one over. Five minutes later, he took the discussion a stage further.

'Do you really think the overall situation would be improved if you took the parcel and I went on to Cotton-wood to try and set up a trap for the collectors?'

'Sure, I do. I really think it would. In fact, it's the sort of move Dick would approve of. I know him well enough to be sure of that. We could put faked notes in the parcel, if you wanted. I would have suggested that before, but I didn't want to give you any new worries.'

The rancher hurriedly shook his head. 'No, Slim, I don't think that would be wise. After all, they might get the parcel opened early in the proceedings, like you suggested, an' if they found wads of newspaper that could be fatal for Red, and possibly for Dick, too. So let's stick to the proper parcel an' work it out from there.'

Slim said rather absently, 'I'll take

this letter back to the mail office before morning, and collect it in the ordinary way, using your note of authority, during tomorrow morning. That's jest in case we're being watched by somebody here in town.

'Now, about goin' along to the coach with the parcel. If I'm right about the messenger boy bein' eliminated, there's nothing in the rules to suggest I can't try and protect myself. So how could I best do that?'

'A waistcoat!' Vargo spoke so hurriedly that he coughed on smoke. Slim grinned easily at his discomfort and patted him on the back.

'I think I know what you mean, Mr. Vargo, a waistcoat padded in such a way as to stop bullets. Is that it? Me, I was thinkin' along the same lines, but favourin' a frockcoat. Ain't never wore one in my life before, but a frockcoat has a whole lot more cloth in it than a waistcoat, an' I thought it would offer a whole lot more protection.'

Vargo at once warmed to the idea of

a long padded coat. He thought that if the padding was overdone it might be rather too heavy for comfort, and therefore it could slow the wearer down. But it was still a good suggestion, and the rancher gave the name of a man in town discreet enough to produce such a garment in next to no time, if the note of authority was shown.

The older man grew morose again as he considered once again where his nephew, Red, might be imprisoned. Slim squatted on his haunches against a wall and put his thoughts back to what had happened before time and a pressing appointment with the newspaper editor drew him to this town.

'There's no doubt in my mind that Red is somewhere between Medicine Creek and Cottonwood. From what I could find out before I left Medicine, they both were headed Cottonwood way, and Red, who seems to have been laying a trail, masquerading as Dick, deliberately spread it around that he was going by the longer route, that is, the loop. Known as Indian Gulch. Somewhere along the trail, Red dropped out of circulation. And Dick seems to have done the same.

'Me, I rode across the more direct trail between the two towns an' explored that wilderness of hills an' valleys to the north an' east of the most obvious kidnap spot, an' although I came up with nothing, I obviously disturbed someone in the area who had taken a great deal of trouble to stay out of sight during the day. In shooting up my bed roll his motive could not have been robbery. He must have wanted me out of the way because I was exploring in a place where others didn't want me pryin'. So I'd say something's definitely brewin' over there.

'It could be the hideout spot for a kidnapped man, or, it might even be the rendezvous for undesirables, comin' from the west. Who can tell? I would say that whichever it is it ought to be looked into, an' the man to put that in motion is the one with the most prestige in the district.'

'Meanin' me,' Vargo put in, with a chuckle. He came off the bed and padded across the floor to the chest of drawers. From the top one he took a folded map and tossed it across to Slim. 'Take a look at that. It might interest you.'

Slim caught the map and unfolded it with growing interest. It was not new. Something stamped on one corner suggested that it had been printed twenty years ago. Cottonwood and Medicine were small, comparatively new settlements in those days. What finally crystallised his interest was a pencil ring around a special place in the area which they had been discussing.

The younger man came hurriedly to his feet. He crossed to the hanging lamp in the centre of the room and there perused the map in the best light. The small print inside the ring was clearly visible to his first rate eyesight.

He read out: 'Bonanza M. H.

Company. Now ain't that a coincidence?'

Vargo was vigorously shaking his
head. 'I don't think it is a coincidence.
By what you tell me, you must have
almost stumbled upon those old mine
workings before that man shot up your
bed roll.

'Kidnappers, for my money, have
more than their fair share of vicious-
ness, but they don't have a lot of
imagination. Whoever concocted this
devilish plan to separate me from
twenty thousand dollars had to think up
an address of some sort. If I'm not
mistaken, he's been fool enough to give
away the location of his base!'

Slim whistled. 'So now we know
where to look, an' where to direct the
county peace officers, if they'll only play
ball an' help us.'

The excitement fired both men for
another ten minutes. Slim, oddly
enough, was the first to show signs of
extreme tiredness. Vargo insisted that he
should sleep on the bed for a few hours.

Before the ordinary townsfolk began to use the street, the younger man was roused again so that he could resume his interrupted vigil at the mail office before the ordinary day staff appeared.

When he left the hotel, he had with him a small compact parcel.

14

At ten a.m. on the Thursday in question there was quite a lot of the usual good-humoured chitchat in the street where the stagecoach loaded for the run to Cottonwood. Two men and three women boarded it, and had their baggage stowed in the boot. A man from a bank brought a couple of small items for the strong box and waited while it was locked and secured.

The horses, a fine team of six, grew restless. So did Slim Petersen who was closely watching everything that went on from a distance of fifty yards. Slim felt hot and he perspired a lot in clothes which he was not used to. He had been very busy in the time since Raich Vargo had slipped away towards Cottonwood. Now, his anxiety was building up to a climax. He felt as if he was being set up for kidnap, as Red had been. But his probable fate was more short-lived; so he did not dwell upon it.

He watched the coach swing out into the dirt with the driver hauling on his reins and calling to the team to start pulling. At that moment, he did not feel at all keen on his special assignment. He would much rather have been ploughing, or digging, or even branding Walter Legrange's few head of cattle.

Walter, Maria and the Nester Valley seemed an age away. He wondered what fate would do to him in the next few hours, and whether he would get back to see those who needed him most. He knew then, for the first time, that his appointed task in life, if he had one, was out there in Nester Valley, alongside Walter and Maria, making a worthwhile life out of that rich soil. It was an opportunity which few modest young men would turn down.

Soon, the coach was out of sight and only chatting bystanders and a faint pall of dust bore witness to where it had been. Slim became impatient. He made a last visit to his hotel room and settled his last few bits of business. By the time he was headed out of town in the coach's wake, he figured that it had a lead of two miles.

★　★　★

An hour after midday, the vehicle started to approach the small settlement known as Halfway Creek. Slim, resplendent in his grey frockcoat and holed side-rolled hat, began to overtake it. Some three quarters of a mile short of the buildings he pushed the dun alongside of the coach, and signalled for the driver to stop.

The shotgun guard waved the standard weapon in his direction. The driver remained watchful and alert. It was only when the men in the back of the coach, who were armed, decided that the meeting was an innocent one that the driver complied with Slim's request.

Many pairs of eyes watched him as

he dipped inside the frockcoat and brought out the parcel. The guard, who was long-sighted, held it at arm's length while he read out the address upon it.

He said: 'There'll be a special charge for stoppin' the coach at an irregular stop, young fellow, but we can't rightly refuse to deliver your parcel, if it's all that important to you. Let's see, three dollars might cover it, I guess.'

Slim grinned and nodded. He had the money ready, and he passed it over without delay. He thought fleetingly that these ordinary travellers watching his every move might be the last people to see him alive. And, having duly frightened himself, he then touched his hat and put his spurs to the dun, which rapidly took him ahead.

He was remembering his instructions, and he intended to carry them out to the letter. The quickest and easiest way to get off the track was on the north side. Consequently, he put the dun at a low hogsback ridge on the south side and did not stop pushing it until they were over the highest point and beginning to adjust for the descent.

Some little distance below, he glimpsed water. A quick glance through his spy glass showed where two men were resting their horses on a wooden trestle bridge about four hundred yards away. Short of that there was no obvious spot where a rider might easily be ambushed.

His observation showed that they were looking in a different direction. They were, in fact, looking for a rider to come round the west end of the ridge and so link up with the route they were on.

Slim took the bridge as the danger spot. Having decided on what was in store for him, he began to act accordingly. He slid the dun down much of the ridge and achieved cover at trail level before he was seen. He went through rough unbroken land on a course converging with the winding trail.

About a hundred and fifty yards from the bridge, he suddenly appeared on the trail. The men on the bridge then showed a little excitement. One of them bent down and began to examine the rear hooves of his horse, as though the animal had cast a shoe or picked up stones.

Slim guessed that this was subterfuge. As the winding trail went round a tree-covered curve, he dropped down to the narrow stream, splashed across it and went on at the same good pace. His direction would take him on beyond the bridge without his having to use it at all. After a couple of minutes his manoeuvre was detected. The rider on the bridge stopped playing about with his horse's hooves and hurriedly mounted up. The two men put themselves on a course which would make their trail cross with Slim's in a matter of about two hundred yards.

Slim thought hard. His own cayuse was far from fresh. In the glimpses of him which showed through the trees he made out that he was hard-pressed and struggling. The other two looked confident. They were only waiting for the

213

range to lessen before they opened up on him.

One last thick crescent of timber lay ahead of the fugitive. He used it and used it well, doing an about turn within its shade. When he reappeared, he had gone away from the other two, and he took the dun alongside the side of the stream and under the bridge itself.

The two-man pursuit team was baffled for a time. Slim made ground. He was just beginning to think that he might have thrown them off for good when a rifle opened up on him from a miniature copse about seventy yards to his right. Bullets flew near, and one actually hit him below his left shoulder.

The shock of this almost bowled him out of the saddle, but he hung on, and survived another direct hit in the back which again proved the efficiency of the padded coat. Fifty yards further on, he dismounted in a hollow. By making detours and varying his rate of progress he succeeded in throwing off those who should have killed him inside two hours.

★ ★ ★

The hours of darkness that night were few. Slim gave himself an extra hour before nightfall to get together his camp and he took a half hour after dawn to see to his simple needs and break it. He threw away his invaluable padded frockcoat after using it for an extra night blanket, thinking that it might impede his progress on what he took to be one of the critical days of his life.

Raich Vargo's old map had been accurate. Around ten in the morning, Slim came out upon a high point which had once been the limit of an overhead ore truck railway. From there, he was able to see a long way in all directions.

Some few miles to the westward, a pall of dust seemed to suggest moving people. A vehicle or a bunch of riders. Whichever it was the dust cloud was coming nearer. A mere few hundred yards way was a natural basin which had been the working encampment of the old mine.

As he watched he saw two armed men who occasionally came out from a hole in a low cliff, as though they were guarding someone inside there. His spirits lifted, in spite of his weariness. He knew his enemies and the enemies of the Vargos were numerically superior. Some had tried to kill him near Halfway Creek. Others would have to go to Cottonwood on this day to collect the all-important parcel, and here, almost within striking distance were two more.

It also occurred to him that the moving dust cloud might be reinforcements. Even possibly the vicious bunch of renegades mentioned in the local press. He wondered if Doublejack Murphy was one of them, and he knew that if he was to save the prisoner, or prisoners, he had to act quickly before any of the others returned to base.

He paused just long enough to slake the thirst of the dun and himself and then he was on the move again. He turned north, away from the edge of the work arena and made a slight detour, looking for some other way into the cliff from which the ore had been excavated. He found that the cliff of the higher ground was in the shape of a horseshoe and that round the nearer extremity there was an external passage running straight up to a part of the cliff with a gap in it.

Maybe that gap was the answer to his wishes. Half an hour later, he was down in the gap, having abandoned the dun on the higher ground. He entered the gap, moving with caution, and found himself in a minor tunnel, the props of which were in poor repair. There had been falls since the place closed down, and only this desperate emergency made Slim want to face the hazards in there at all.

He lost two matches in quick succession. The second one went out when a furry animal frightened him. He took it to be a rat, and when he cautiously investigated the place, he had a stroke of luck. He came upon an old wax candle which was in perfectly good condition.

Aided by the flickering light, which needed a lot of shielding with his hand, he made upwards of a hundred yards' progress, and only slowed down when he started to hear voices. He spent a lot of time in studying the layout of the tunnel just ahead of him, and noted where the turn came in it before nipping out the candle for greater safety.

He moved more slowly then, and it became clear that he was moving into the rear of a small party.

'Hey, Butch, will you stay awake for a while? I can't be alert all the time, an' you know it. Since you made that trip to Thompson you've been nothing but a liability. Why, twice you've dropped off while I've been sleepin' an' if Vargo back there had anywhere to go he could have broken out an' been lost to us forever. Doggone it, what did you have to drink while you were in town?'

'All right, all right, Jake, but don't

keep on about it. I'll go take a walk in the fresh air. Maybe it's that stale air in the mine workings that's gettin' me down.'

A figure, which was perhaps thirty yards way from Slim, detached itself from the ground and sauntered towards the big opening beyond, taking a rifle with him. The silhouette of the man who had been arguing with him showed lower down, as though he was seated with his back to a rock, against the side of the tunnel.

There was only one armed man ahead of Slim now, and he moved forward, determined to take his chance with the fellow. Some ten yards further on, on hands and knees, he sensed that someone else was there, and that his presence was known.

Dick Vargo, reclining near the other wall, and much closer than the outlaw, cautiously showed himself. The intruder had to work hard to stifle a mild cry of surprise. He edged over towards the prisoner, who was lying on his side, and began to communicate with him.

Dick's eyes were much better adjusted to the dark than Slim's were. He intimated by gestures that he would draw the guard to the back of the tunnel for Slim to deal with. Slim, his heart thumping rather wildly, signified his approval.

Dick called: 'Wagner, can you come here a minute?'

'What in tarnation do you want now, Vargo? Ain't I been fussin' over you ever since we hit this Godforsaken pit? Ain't I?'

Wagner sounded as if he wanted an answer, but he did not get one and presently he scrambled to his feet and wandered back to find out what was bothering the all-important prisoner. Slim stood up and clicked back the hammer of his Colt when he was standing behind Wagner and some ten feet away.

The outlaw recovered with remarkable speed. Instead of stretching up his hands straight away, he dipped for a belt knife and brought up his hand throwing it, all in one smooth movement. Slim had never moved his head so fast before. Fortunately, the blade narrowly missed him and buried its tip in a pit prop just behind him.

Not wanting to blast off his gun and warn the other outlaw, Slim threw himself forward and closed the gap between them. Wagner might have been lifting a gun, but, as it happened he was not. Slim threw a hurried one-two of punches at his chest and forcibly threw him back towards Dick.

The latter at once contrived to trip the guard. Wagner went down with scarcely a sound. Dick rolled on the floor as the body dipped towards him. Something which he held in his two hands behind his back impaled the falling man.

Jake Wagner's face would have been a study, had there been more light in the tunnel. As it was, the single thrust with a rusty knife was sufficient to mortally wound him. He died within a minute, before Slim could fully comprehend how it had happened.

The newcomer bent over the prisoner and cut him free with Wagner's knife. He whispered: 'You had a knife all the time, and yet you didn't attempt to get free before this?'

Dick nodded and grinned sardonically. 'I had my reasons. I wanted my freedom, but I wanted the lives of these two fiends as well. Besides, the knife was rusted up to the hilt. Its cutting edges were no good. But it served a useful purpose jest now.'

Slim wanted to ask about Red, but the time was not yet. Dick massaged his wrists and crawled forward to the mouth of the opening, taking Wagner's rifle with him. This time Slim wanted to take the initiative. He stood back in the entrance until Logan appeared round the side of a small shanty some fifty yards away.

Slim called: 'The game is up, outlaw. Raise your hands, or do the other!'

Having called the warning, Slim dropped to the ground and levelled his

Winchester. Butch, of course, did the other. He dropped his rifle and grabbed for his matched six-guns. Both of them cleared leather and started to point on target, but ahead of him the two rifles blasted off, and he fired into the dirt.

His body jerked one way and then the other, and finally crumpled to the ground. Slim was the first to get up. He crossed to the fallen man and saw that both rifle bullets had entered his chest and either of them would have killed him.

Slim was not altogether pleased. He said: 'You didn't intend to give him any sort of chance, Dick. You fired almost before I'd done speaking.'

Dick turned away from the corpse. 'That's right, Slim. Red is dead, thanks to these two hombres, an' he didn't die prettily.'

Slim regretted his words, and said so. They shook hands.

15

The stagecoach from Thompson Falls
arrived in Cottonwood that same day,
on the second leg of its journey around
noon. Various interested and disinter-
ested spectators watched the travellers
and saw the baggage unloaded. Within
half an hour, the mail was in the mail
office and the valuables carried in the
treasure box had been distributed.

Lucky Parradine had taken a bath
and visited the barber's since his arrival
in town for the all-important pick-up.
He sauntered along to the mail office,
trying to give the impression of being
a well heeled stranger in town on
business.

Cottonwood's mail office was simi-
larly appointed to the one in Thompson.
Lucky saw that it had been newly painted.
He hoped the paint face-lift was a good
omen for the future. Before he walked

into the office on the first floor from the staircase, he glanced down into the street and eyed two men who were loitering about there. One of them had three horses by him and was casually rocking saddles. The other was some twenty yards away, looking as if he had no connection with the horse-minder, just in case anything went wrong and they needed a diversion.

Putting a smile on his olive-skinned hirsute face, Lucky said: 'Howdy, mister, I'm an official of the Bonanza Mine Holdings Company, based in Sante Fe. I was instructed to come here an' collect a small parcel addressed to my organisation care of this office. May I ask if it has arrived yet? Coming from the county seat, I think.'

The veteran clerk nodded pleasantly enough. He shambled across to the rack where the parcels of medium size were kept and picked out the one with the required address on it. Glancing over the top of his spectacles at Parradine, and two other men who were loafing about the room, he returned with it.

'I guess this must be what you're lookin' for, sir. I'll have to ask you to sign for it. Right here.'

While Parradine's fingers were busy with the pen, a gun dug gently into his backbone. The man who had been standing further away stepped forward and removed his weapons, giving him a very thorough search at the same time.

'I protest at this outrage!' Parradine blustered, two spots of high colour forming in his cheeks.

He looked as if he was going to try and make a dash for the door but his captors dissuaded him. As soon as the three of them appeared at the top of the stairs, the horse minder and the observer stiffened up and went for their guns.

Raich Vargo, who had been sitting on a bench across the street, pretending to be asleep, came to his feet and menaced the horse-minder with a gun from the rear. The town marshal, who stepped out of an alley, did not act so delicately.

He brought his gun down on the back of the other man's head. Two part-time constables, along with the deputies from the mail office, took over the prisoners.

Moustached Town Marshal Coots greeted Vargo with a forked-tooth grin: 'That suit you for prompt action, Mr. Vargo?'

'Sure, sure, marshal, that was great, take them along an' hold them. I'll be along to prefer charges later. Very shortly, I'll be ridin' out of town towards the south. I want to make contact with that posse the deputy sheriff took out to try an' locate the latest bunch of raiders. I don't think I've got much to keep me here, right now.'

The marshal remarked upon the rancher's ability to get around at speed, and shortly afterwards, left with the arrested men. The mail office clerk came out into the open and tossed down the parcel. Raich Vargo caught it and opened it.

'That's it, sure enough,' he called up,

with a sigh of relief. 'I'll come up an' see you when I get back to town, Jose!'

The clerk signalled that he had heard and understood, and ten minutes later, the rancher rode out of town and turned south.

★ ★ ★

Earlier that morning, Doublejack Murphy, a big bent-nosed ruffian of doubtful parentage with an insatiable desire to hurt and rob, had been running amok along a placid creek, west of the mine site, along with four veteran outlaws who had joined up with him as soon as he was released.

At the first pioneer homestead, a young son of a large family had been shot dead. An hour later, at the next settlement, a girl had suffered a shoulder wound because she was slow to comply with their orders. A small boy had since slipped away from this homestead on a pregnant mule to inform the authorities in distant Cottonwood.

By far the worst showing of all by these wild hellions was the shooting up of four new shops perhaps half a mile away from the creek, where determined settlers were trying to start a new town. Two men and one woman were shot to death within their premises without a proper chance to defend themselves or to surrender. The raiders spent an hour there, eating and drinking and taking whatever they needed for their own requirements.

At last, they were tired, but they were not fools enough to relax near the places they had plundered. They came away, and did not settle themselves down to rest until they had put two miles between them and the devastated shops.

After an hour, Doublejack was on his feet, walking up and down and cautiously dry-trimming his chin stubble with a cut-throat razor acquired that morning.

'Come on, come on, you hellions, I don't like this area. I don't like it at all! Let's make tracks for the old mine. There's a place where a man can rejoin his old buddies an' feel safe while he rests! What do you say, boys?'

None of the four boys so addressed had any special inclination to rouse out and move on, but they had far too much sense to go against their leader, who had been known for many years on account of his hair-trigger temper.

They all said they were ready, and five minutes later, headed by the formidable ex-jailbird, they rode off on the last leg of their journey to the old base.

★　★　★

Slim and Dick had a whole lot to talk about. They exchanged information over a leisurely meal, and put off as long as they could the disposal of the two outlaws' bodies. Slowly they walked around the work arena, studying the old warehouse, the office and the bunkhouse. Red's untimely death was the topic which troubled them the most, and after talking about it in some detail, they avoided it thereafter.

Tucked away in a corner of the arena was an unexpected find. Judging by the names on the head boards of the dead, it was the graveyard of old working mules which had died in harness. As they studied it, the same kind of thoughts went through both heads.

Dick enquired: 'Do you feel that we owe Wagner an' Logan a lot of respect at a time like this?'

'No, I don't,' Slim answered quickly. 'I figure they were a menace in any community an' that we've done this county a service in gettin' rid of them. I think this patch of ground will serve quite well as a last restin' place for them. Is that your conclusion?'

Dick nodded and grinned rather unpleasantly. Speeding up a little, they returned to the place where the bodies were waiting and covered and transported them to the burial spot with the aid of outlaw horses. The digging would have seemed interminable for one man, but for these two, working side by side and egging one another on, gradually the double-sized pit was prepared.

Just before the burial, they paused long enough to take stock of their present position. Slim had explained his view of the situation earlier, but Dick, not very fresh after his incarceration in the mine, had clearly not taken it all in.

Slim slowly scratched his bare chest. 'Three groups could make it to us here, Dick. Firstly, there's those who went to Cottonwood to collect your father's money. They're almost bound to come here, unless they've been jumped in town. Then there's this Wild Bunch, who may be much nearer than we think, seein' as how I saw a cloud of dust, on the way in here. An' then there's an outside possibility of a posse operatin' in this area on the advice of your father.'

Dick shifted his weight, which was resting on the handle of his shovel. 'Two hostile groups out of three. We could possibly take the money collectors by surprise, if we were properly organised and ready. I'm not so sure about the other jaspers, though, the ones who are supposed to be operatin' west of here.

'If two hostile groups showed up, which we can fully expect, we might be in trouble. What if the posse doesn't show up at all?'

Slim frowned. 'As you say, we could be in a fix. But I take it you would risk stayin' here a little longer, if only to try an' recover your Pa's money?'

'If you put it that way, amigo, I'd be willin' to stay here for jest one more night. So let's get these two stiffs interred an' make plans for other eventualities, huh?'

Slim was thinking that it was high time one or other of them moved out on to high ground and took a long look at the surrounding terrain, but he kept his impatience in check and went to work again with the spade.

Before the corpses were actually buried he studied the calloused hand which had wielded the tomahawk.

16

Deputy Sheriff Ray Philson, of Clovis County, was not a popular man in Cottonwood, the town from which the ten posse riders had been brought. He was a tall, narrow-shouldered, red-faced ex-cavalry N.C.O. with a waxed grey moustache which made him look a little older than his forty years.

At two in the afternoon, his men were resting in the comparative shade of a rather arid hollow a short distance to the east of the mine workings. They had now suffered several hours of protracted riding in a day of intense heat, and they had seen nothing at all to make them believe that their ride was going to be productive.

Philson knew that they were on the point of a group protest. He had walked away from them, ostensibly to survey the surrounding land. As it was there was no high point near at hand to help him to any worthwhile conclusion, but he learned a whole lot more about their private feelings from what he overheard on his return.

One man was saying: 'Old Ramrod Philson thinks he's still in the army, pardner. He don't think that this day's ride will do any good, any more than we do, but he's a stickler for his duty, an' he'll keep us at it, sweltering in the sun, until nightfall. An' we all have work waitin' for us elsewhere.'

'Maybe he thinks that if we run across that old reprobate Doublejack Murphy an' drive him into the next county, some friend of the territorial governor will pin a medal on him. If you want my private opinion, I think he's nuts!'

Philson flushed and ground his teeth together. He had long since learned that an eavesdropper never hears good of himself. He stomped up the slope to rejoin his men in a filthy mood. Just in case they had cotton wool in their ears he cleared his throat rather noisily to warn them of his approach.

As it happened, a former miner, who had his back to the deputy, had been deafened by an explosion at an earlier age. He did not hear the posse leader's approach. Unfortunately, he chose that moment to give his opinion.

'If you boys ask me, the army hasn't yet produced a peace officer who is properly cut out for the job! No, sir, neither the Yankees nor the Johnnie Rebs!'

All the other men knew of Philson's approach. There was little he could do about the last expression of opinion. He walked among the mildly embarrassed posse men with a very straight face.

'Well, boys, it begins to look as if today ain't our lucky day. Maybe tomorrow we'll have better luck. I guess we ought to hit the saddles in the next few minutes.'

His riders, all of whom had expected to be home that evening, were outraged by the news that they might have to spend the night in the open. They all stood up, all around him, waiting for one another to protest. Philson, however, was wearing his most dominating, frigid expression, and the protest somehow remained unuttered.

Four hundred yards short of the mine arena, Doublejack Murphy, christened Sean, held up his hand and halted the forward progress of his diminutive band. He, for his part, looked them over and decided they were a sorry crew to have as bodyguard for a gang leader who looked upon himself as the Scourge of the southwest. The youngest among them was thirty-nine years of age. One had a beard which looked like a lump of tumbleweed stuck on. Sean was tactful enough not to reveal his thoughts, but he secretly hoped that the men already assembled in the mine would be more presentable, that they would look formidable, and that they would know how to treat a returning leader.

What he wanted was a kind of

triumphal entry to this scene of his former triumphs. While he brooded, an idea occurred to him. He waved his arm for the riders to bunch.

'Boys, I want you to ride towards the mine in a straight line, an' when I give the signal put your guns in the air an' fire off a salvo of welcome!'

Some of his hearers were astute enough to know that the salvo of welcome ought to have come from those already entrenched at the mine, but again, they kept their thoughts to themselves. Fifty yards short of the great work area, the line halted. The guns were raised and all firearms, rifles and revolvers were discharged into the air.

Two horses played up and were instantly savaged with rowels and short whips. As the pall of gunsmoke gradually drifted away the sudden quietness disturbed the newcomers. They began to glance openly at one another, wondering if all was well.

A big, noisy welcome was not necessary, but they would have liked to be assured that their friends were ensconced at the place and that everything was prepared for them. Nothing happened to boost their confidence.

The continued silence affected Murphy's nerves. He galloped forward alone and only pulled up when he was near the edge of the drop. His grey stallion twitched its ears and tossed its head while he glanced beyond it, looking for signs of humans. He had the feeling that someone was there, but there was not much of a tangible nature to go on.

An imperious wave brought the rest of his group to him. They lined up with him, two on either side, watchful and suspicious.

'What do you make of it, Doublejack?' the bearded ruffian to his right enquired.

'I think we have someone here, but it's hard to tell. There's a small heap of something over there, beyond the mine entrance. Can you tell from here if it's fresh manure?'

Two men decided that it was. They

split up, after that, and entered the lower level at the corners on the west side. Individual riders raced here and there as though the discovery of an interloper was a matter of life and death.

Murphy stayed near the west side, in front of the warehouse. Presently, the others came out into the centre area, shrugging and still watchful.

'No men in evidence at all?' Murphy queried. Each man shook his head. 'Well, there's five horses in that warehouse. All good ridin' horses, an' that has to mean something.'

A man who rejoiced under the name of China Joe remarked: 'There's a burial spot over the corner back there. The earth's been turned quite recently. It's kind of big for one man, as well. A man don't dig more than he has to, especially out in the wilds, like this is.'

In a group, they inspected the burial ground. They agreed with China Joe's findings. After that, they dismounted, took their weapons and worked their way with great deliberation from one end of the camp to the other.

Apart from the droppings, the riding horses and the new grave, nothing further had come to light. Murphy smoked with his back to the small office, hidden from the mine entrance by its wall.

'Boys, there's men about here. One thing is clear, they ain't friends, otherwise they'd have shown themselves. So it's the other kind, an' we know where they have to be. They ain't gone any place without them fine horses.'

'Inside the mine, Boss?' Stride asked. He was the man with the beard.

'That's right, an' we have to get them out an' find out what's been happening before we can consider settlin' in here for any length of time. So we're goin' to be busy for a while. This time it ain't goin' to be quite so easy. I want you to spread yourselves out so that you can get in some good shots at the mine opening. Get about your business now. I'm impatient.'

Three minutes later, he made his

pronouncement. 'You men inside that mine, I want you to come out here. If you don't keep me waitin' nothin' much is goin' to happen to you. You have a choice.'

Slim and Dick whispered to each other in the darkness. They knew they were in for a rough time. Murphy's promise of leniency did not impress them at all.

Dick replied: 'If you're talkin' to us, mister, we ain't listenin'. We came in here of our own accord an' we don't want to talk with you. As a matter of fact, you make too much noise.'

Murphy fumed. He was faced with a man, or possibly anything up to five men, and he was being defied. He thought of the havoc he had caused earlier that day, and he wished he could make the man who had replied aware of it.

After a pause, he called: 'All right, suit yourself, mister!'

Ten seconds later, all five men were peppering the entrance with their shoulder weapons. The air was full of the hiss and whine of flying lead. Dirt and chipped stone flew up. The yawning gap at which they were aiming was far from healthy.

There had been no reply, either verbally or with firearms. In the depths behind the entrance, the two men were muffling their coughs with bandannas so that no sound at all came from the workings. The attackers were baffled. Murphy felt certain that this quietness did not mean the opposition was knocked out. He felt sure that it was a staged quietness; the men inside were testing his patience.

One thing he could not stand, after being imprisoned for so long, was a job which got on his nerves. He called to the man with the yellowish complexion, China Joe, who retired to his horse, unimpeded, and returned with a stick of dynamite.

China Joe wriggled right up to his Boss and made known the shortcomings of this particular explosive. 'It's a little past its best, an' the fuse, as you can see, is very short. It'll have to be handled with great care.'

Murphy nodded. He handled the stick gingerly, waited to see if China would volunteer to throw it, and then reluctantly assumed the responsibility of handling it himself. Joe went back to his own spot, and awaited developments. Two minutes went by, during which Murphy changed his mind about immediate tactics.

Although he and his men were out in the open, in the daylight, he decided that they should gradually move in upon the entrance and take the opposition without use of the explosive. He signified what he wanted done by a series of hand waves and gestures.

He fired three bullets himself to start the manoeuvre. Soon, regular rifle shots were echoing round the arena area, and the deadly intruders were worming their way steadily nearer. The attackers had little cover, other than an occasional small rock, but the smoke that eddied in the area made it difficult for the defenders to get a clear view of them.

Slim and Dick fired every now and then from positions about five yards apart to check the attackers' advance, but after ten minutes, Stride, the bearded man, leapt to his feet five yards out and hurled himself into the entrance.

The defenders' two shoulder weapons were both discharged at the same time. Stride arched his back, in a posture he had not used for years. He stiffened still more, twisted in the air and finally flopped across the entrance.

Another man came two minutes later, running from the opposite side, but Slim, who had crept forward to wait behind the corpse, easily picked him off, sending him to the ground about three yards out. Murphy called a halt and the gunfire died for a time.

Dick came up alongside of his partner and offered a word of congratulation about Slim's last effort. He asked what sort of a change was made, and received only a shrug by way of reply. They knew that the breathing space could only mean some other attack of a more deadly form.

For another minute, they watched the two men whom they could just see beyond the vision-limiting sides of the entrance. Dick gave a sudden gasp and pointed in the direction of the man in the dark suit. This was Murphy, himself.

'He's gettin' ready to throw something, Slim. A dynamite stick, or I'm off my head! Let's get back as far as we can!'

Without hesitation, they both stood up and made a rush for the rear. No bullets followed them, but presently the spluttering candle came flying through the air, dropped a yard short of Stride's body and slowly rolled under it.

No sooner was it still than it exploded. Stride's body was hurled against the roof like a dummy. A blinding flash of flame which changed from bright orange to almost silver illuminated the myriad crevices of the tunnel's walls and ceiling. The ear-splitting sound rolled around the encompassing area and thumped hard at the senses of the two prostrate men, although they had their hands over their ears.

One wall cracked. Two lumps of rock slithered sideways and soil was pumped out from beyond them until there was an untidy heap some three feet in height all the way across the opening. The air was hot and breathing was very difficult. As soon as the booming echoes started to grow quieter, Slim crept across to Dick and tapped him on the shoulder. 'Are you all right, amigo?'

Dick nodded. He sat up, shook the earth off him and felt around to make sure that his weapons were intact. 'My head's singing but I guess I can't complain. What's next?'

'They'll rush us in a short time. We have to make a move before they do.'

'I dont' fancy usin' that wall of stone

and rubble as a barricade. Why, that lunatic might throw another explosive at us!'

'It might not come to that,' Slim surmised. 'After all, I got in here without usin' the main entrance. I suppose I could find my way out again if I had to.'

They both stood erect, listening hard and worrying a little about the outcome.

17

Deputy Sheriff Philson, like any other peace officer, had his weaknesses, but when it came to planning anything definite, like how to surround an old mining area temporarily controlled by a small handful of renegades, he had his moments.

The earlier shooting, when the guns were fired into the air, had been sufficient to alert his men and kill a lot of the grumbling. The later shooting, when the bullets were aimed against humans, merely served to speed the transformed posse in the right direction.

The posse arrived above the arena just before the incident of the dynamite stick. It was eminently clear that the men attacking the mine entrance were renegades. Philson made up his mind quickly. He sent three of his best mounted men around the southern extremity of the arena to take up positions on the heights around the west side.

As soon as they had departed, another pair were sent off to the north side, to achieve a dominating position above the cliffs. The rest were spaced out along the east and south sides of the area. When he was ready, he made sure that he was in a prominent place before shouting his challenge.

'You men down there, this is Deputy Sheriff Philson of Clovis County talkin' to you! I have reason to believe that you are breakers of the law, an' I call upon you to throw down your arms an' surrender to my men who are coming down to your level!'

Murphy, and the two men with him, who had just been about to make a cautious entry of the mine, looked much reduced in the open space down below. In the bright sunlight it was possible to note each man's minutest reactions. There was a hurried consultation. Murphy decided against a protest when he saw the continuous ring of posse riders. Instead, he ordered his men to pick up every available weapon and make a dash into the mine.

Philson noted the move as he gave his moustache a twist. He signalled for his men to get down below by the nearest means of entry, and himself started down the path ahead of him. Seconds later, a rifle fired inside the mine.

On all sides, the advancing posse riders stiffened, straining to see what had happened. Those whose view was a good one saw Doublejack Murphy and China Joe come back out of the mine with their hands in the air. Only two men out of three. Probably the third had objected to throwing down his weapons.

Slim and Dick came out a few seconds later with their weapons trained and steady. Dick had disposed of the other man.

★　★　★

Raich Vargo arrived about fifteen minutes too late to take part in the action. He had to take the punishing news of his nephew's untimely death, but he was clearly delighted to find that Dick had not suffered in any permanent way.

The two young partners and the ageing rancher took a stroll around the mine working arena, swopping information and gradually getting to know one another better. Slim noted that in the talk he was being accepted as an equal almost as a member of the family.

Raich looked them both over and decided that the time was ripe to unburden himself of a family secret. He found a shady spot behind the warehouse and invited his audience to sit down.

'You both know that in the past my brother, Gil, was so far misguided as to ride the owlhoot trail. At one time, I can tell you that it worried me an awful lot. I never knew a proper night's sleep for years. It was then that my hair started to change colour.

'Somehow or another he managed to

stay out of prison, and on the occasions when units of the gang ran into trouble, he was scarcely ever there. As a result of his remarkable run of luck, his Boss, rumour had it that it might have been this Murphy fellow, decided to entrust him with looking after a certain bag of loot directly after the snatch.

'Well, as it happened, the peace officers came off best in that little shoot-out and the racin' an' chasin' which followed broke up the gang so that it was never quite the same again. Gil hid out for a while, an' then decided that he could not stick it any more, so he came home to the Diamond V, determined to settle down.

'I took him at his word, but I didn't rush him. For a time, he stayed at the ranch house with us. And later, he went off to the other end of our territory and tried to devote himself to building up that little place which he left to Red. Before he went, he had something to do.

'He crept out one night and buried

something across the yard. I didn't cotton on to the fact that he was out until he had nearly finished. If I hadn't seen the tools he used the next day, I might have thought it was all a dream.

'Anyways, there was a lot of unhealthy talk in the towns, especially around the saloons, about some loot which Gil Vargo was sittin' on. Gil never mentioned it, an' I never questioned him. He wasn't much cut out for ranchin' or farmin' but at least he stayed at home.

'I didn't mind what men were sayin' except that they hinted that my ranch was bein' built up on stolen money. That hurt me a bit, but I think I lived it down. For years, we lived with the idea that renegades might come back to try and get this loot, if it really existed. Somehow they never reached us, and then Gil died.

'A few months ago, we had a violent thunder storm. Lightning struck a fence post across the yard and knocked it out of the ground. When the weather improved a bit I went out myself to see about putting the post back. It was then I found the old bag of loot. All bills which had suffered through being underground.'

Raich broke off and started to chuckle. Clearly he had some special revelation, something unexpected.

When he was more composed, he resumed: 'The bills were useless. When they were snatched they must have been on their way from the United States treasury to a bank. Anyway, they lacked the signature of the president, and that of the bank treasurer as well.

'So they could never have been spent by the gang. Not unless they were prepared to forge the names of two important people. And I can't see any of Murphy's cronies bein' intelligent enough to do that!'

Slim laughed first, and presently Dick joined in. Laughter did them a deal of good after the tension which they had lived with for so long. Slim was the one who came out with the bright remark. 'So, in a manner of speakin' Gil Vargo did his fellow renegades a good turn when he put that useless money out of circulation. He stopped them from gettin' caught by tryin' to pass money that was useless.'

The Vargos, father and son, laughed some more, and they only started to sober up when they noticed the procession of posse riders weaving their way out of the arena with Murphy and his henchman in their midst.

When the renegades and their escort had gone out of sight, on their way to Cottonwood and a further spell in jail, Slim and the Vargos came together and cooked up a small meal, which they ate out in the open.

By the time Raich got to the tooth picking stage, they were all three getting a little restless to be out of the arena.

Raich said: 'Slim, you look like a good man between jobs. You've got some money comin' from me, but we wouldn't like that to be the end. We could use a good permanent hand high up in our little organisation. What do you say?'

Slim wriggled with embarrassment. He grinned sheepishly at Dick, and then looked away. Thinking he wanted more inducement, Raich went on: 'You could have the house an' the land at the far end of our territory. Where Gil and Red used to live. There's only an oldish woman there, an' she'd be happy to act as housekeeper for you.'

It was obvious by Dick's expression that he wanted Slim to take up the offer, but still the freckle-faced young man wavered. He could see that he would have to make an effort to explain.

'Don't think I don't appreciate your generous offer, Mr. Vargo, because I do. All my workin' life I've been searchin' out a ranchin' family I could look up to an' respect for a long time, an' now I've found one. But, at the same time, I've jest realised that there are two people I'm indebted to from the past. A man who raised me, an' a girl who grew up almost like a sister to me. They live together on a homestead in Nester Valley.

'If they want me there, I'll have to stay there, perhaps permanently. However, if they decided that they wanted a change from Nester Valley, maybe I could persuade them to sell out an' come with me over to your place. In which case I'd be glad to throw in my hand with you, an 'take up those offers of work an' accommodation. So let's leave it at that, an' part the best of friends.'

The Vargos agreed. Presently they rode out together and parted company after warm handshakes. When they were beyond hailing distance Raich gave it as his opinion that Slim would stay in Nester Valley.

'He's in love with that girl back there. She'll hold him to the valley. But never mind. One day, maybe we can loan him the money to expand. Real money. Not Uncle Gil's unsigned variety.'

Dick chuckled, and unselfishly hoped that Slim would make the best choice for himself. When he turned to look back, Slim was already out of sight.